CALLIE'S EMBERS

Fires of Cricket Bend, Book Three

BY MARIE PIPER

CALLIE'S EMBERS

Limitless Publishing, LLC
Kailua, HI 96734
www.limitlesspublishing.com

Formatting: Limitless Publishing

ISBN-13: 978-1-64034-001-5
ISBN-10: 1-64034-001-7

DEDICATION

For Annie

CHAPTER ONE

East Texas, September 1888.

Callie

Clouds as dark as sin lay to the west, just on the horizon. The dark mounds crept slow, threatening and building as if they were waiting for something. Waiting for what, Callie Lee didn't know. As she stood outside her saloon, she watched as they edged inch by inch toward the town of Cricket Bend.

In just another minute she'd go inside and prepare for a storm—move a few of the tables away from the swinging doors, close and bolt the shutters on the windows, and warn the men drinking inside that if they wanted to beat the storm they better get home.

For one more moment, though, she was going to stand and watch.

The air smelled earthy, like coming rain. A feeling in her bones told Callie something more than a storm was coming. Sometimes she had those feelings, prickles on her skin or a pinch in her hip, when something was coming or about to change. Her practical side dismissed it as nothing but hooey, but a small part of her listened.

That small part had whispered so many times over the past eighteen months that Jack Braxton was never coming back to Cricket Bend. The practical side had argued hard—of course he'd come back. He loved her, and they would have a wonderful life together; the life they'd spoken of for a few fleeting months of happiness. She'd argued with herself until she was convinced he was something more than he was.

Jack Braxton was just a man, in the end. He'd died from a gunshot to the chest same as any man would, and that was the end of it. He'd died in a poor town in Tennessee, when the man he'd hunted had become the hunter. The sheriff had found him laying in the middle of the street and the only thing on his person was a note that read *Callie Lee. Cricket Bend, Texas.*

The bastard had known he was going to die, and he hadn't tried to run from it.

The storm grew closer.

"Everything all right, Callie?" The rough voice of Sheriff Luke Anderson caught her attention. He came up beside her on the boardwalk.

They didn't yet know, the rest of the town.

Like Callie, her circle of friends had all thought he'd come back. They'd kept up a relentless hope in his absence. Now Callie alone carried Jack like a burden. She'd been carrying the news for a week now, and the wound still felt fresh.

2

"I'm watching that big cloud over there. The one that looks like the Devil himself."

Luke glanced up at the sky. "Probably gonna be a big one."

"You think a twister?" They'd had one the year before, and it had cost them the roof of the schoolhouse.

"Nah. Not hot enough for that."

"Good," she said. "That's real good."

They'd celebrated the sheriff's fiftieth birthday a few months back, but Luke was still an impressive man. He stood tree-strong and tall, and his dark mustache only showed a few hints of gray. The man was sheriff for good reason, arguably a better person than most anyone else in town, and always there to help. His big brown eyes practically dripped with concern. The man was too damn smart not to notice something wasn't right.

Callie didn't have the heart to tell him that, this time around, there was nothing he could do to help. Her heart was broken, and a big storm was coming.

Luke set a hand on her shoulder. "You and Nate be safe, all right? Take to the cellar if need be. Leave the saloon to ruin if you have to. It's just a building, remember."

Callie looked over her shoulder at the building she owned. Apart from her almost three-year-old son, the saloon was her greatest pride on the earth. The sound of the conversations and music coming from inside made her crack a smile.

"Thank you for the advice, Sheriff." She only ever called him that when she was teasing, and he caught it. No one with any sense would risk their life to save a building. She'd been through a few bad storms during her three years living in Cricket Bend, and knew how bad they could get.

"I best make sure everyone's ready. Find me if you need me."

"I surely will."

He started to go down the steps to the street.

How she wanted to be able to tell him about Jack. Of all the people in the whole town, Luke would get it—he wouldn't push to see how she was doing, wouldn't expect her to break down weeping.

Callie's stomach twisted. Damn Jack Braxton. Damn him to Hell. Damn him from running toward death instead of away from it.

He may not have valued his life enough to fight for it, but there were still an awful lot of days left in Callie's own life. She was going to make them count.

"I think I'll run for mayor."

She called it after him. Luke, at the words, stopped and turned back her way. Callie rushed ahead lest he tell her the idea was foolish. "They elected a woman for mayor in Kansas back in April. Susanna Salter. First female mayor in the whole country. I read about it."

Luke only thought about it for a second. "All right."

"Could I do that here?"

"Don't see why not."

"You think anyone'd be fool enough to vote for me?"

"I think they'd be fools not to. You got my vote, if it matters."

4

"It does." If Luke supported her, there might be a chance she could win. If he supported her, then that likely meant Doc Gray would too, and Deputy Matthew Frank, and a number of others. The saloon patrons, they'd support her.

The whole thing could be just crazy enough to work.

"Good." Her spirit felt a little lighter. "Good."

"You feel like doin' me a favor?"

"Anything, sugar."

"You want to tell Jasper to get inside before the storm hits? Otherwise he's likely to stand staring at you until the wind carries him to California." Luke threw a nod over his shoulder.

Across the street and down a bit, Jasper Tanner stood in front of the Cricket Bend jail. Though the street had plenty of people on it, and the sky was getting darker, his attention was squarely focused on Callie.

This was nothing new. Everyone in Cricket Bend knew by now that Jasper was crazy about her. What they didn't know was that the sight of Jasper made Callie's heart flutter a bit too.

Hearts, after all, were known for their terrible timing.

She bristled. "You're his boss, ain't you? You tell him. I got enough men to worry about, unless you want a bunch of drunks getting lost in a storm."

Turning away before Luke could answer, Callie went back in the saloon. The crowd was quiet that night. Wednesdays weren't peak business, and it wasn't even eight o'clock. The majority of her patrons arrived later, but the looming storm would probably keep many of them at home. The night would likely be calm.

To make her way up the stairs to her suite of rooms, she had to slip through the drinking men. The few of them who were there greeted her warmly, and she paused a moment to chat. Cricket Bend was a small enough town that she knew most all their names and faces, and could truly say she cared about most of them.

Up the saloon stairs was the person she cared most for in the whole of the world.

At two-and-a-half years old and growing every day, Nate blessedly slept like the dead.

How had it been years already? Callie could already barely remember the squalling baby who had turned all the days and nights of his first year into an exhausted blur. Who had time to bother with anything when there was a baby to be fed, rocked, changed, and doted on?

Jeepers, but she loved him.

She rested a hand on his warm forehead and leaned down for a kiss, staying there for a moment with her lips against his soft skin. Sneaking out quietly, she locked the rooms back up again and went back down to the saloon.

How much longer could she keep living above the saloon with a little boy? The rooms were fine, but small, and the kitchen in back of the bar was fine enough for the cooking Callie could do, but Nate was getting bigger every day. With bigger size came more energy, and he'd need more room as he grew. The large staircase that led upstairs was a hazard, and Lord only knew that no matter how hard she tried to keep the peace in her place, sometimes chaos was unavoidable. Sometimes cowboys would come in and get drunk and set a poker table on fire. Sometimes a mean man would try and kill a woman he didn't care for. These things happened in the world, and Callie Lee was determined they would not happen in the same building in which she raised her son.

When Jack had been around, they had talked of building a house together. It would be a fine house, big enough to impress without seeming too snooty. It had been the stuff of dreams, she realized now. Everything they'd shared had been a dream.

After all, when she'd met him, she'd been a whore.

While she'd been good at her trade, the business of pleasure wasn't something a woman could build a life upon. So when her former employer, Hank Porter, had turned tail and run out of Cricket Bend like a thief in the night after getting caught up in things he shouldn't have ever messed with, Callie had purchased the saloon and taken over. She'd traded silk lingerie and bed sheets for inventory, building maintenance, and an all-around respectable position. When Hank had taken off, Callie had seen and seized the chance to change her life. She'd not only taken over ownership of the saloon, she'd made it better, and by doing so found even more success. Cricket Bend was the only real town around for twenty-five miles, and Callie's was the best saloon in farther than that save for the gambling halls in Greeley.

She circled the tables, letting the few men know

that the storm was coming. Most of them stood up and finished their drinks to head home.

One older man, tall and lean with a walrus mustache, stayed leaning on the bar.

"You ridin' it out, Hill?"

"Shoot." He waved a hand. "Rain and thunder don't scare me."

The man had fought in the war, and Callie figured she was in for a spun yarn about how after facing death and looking it in the eye, weather wasn't frightening to Hill Hilton. Not that she minded. Not many men in the world were as kind and reliable as Hill, even if he drank too much.

The rain began to fall outside. It rapped quickly against the glass windows.

"I won't kick you out." Her hand patted Hill's as she came out from behind the bar, headed for the door to get a glimpse of the rain and the severity of the clouds. What were they in for? If the thunder got too loud, she'd likely have a scared child to attend to and might have to close up.

Just as she reached the doors, they swung open and nearly knocked her over.

Jasper stepped inside. His tan duster was already dotted with dark water spots, and he pulled off his hat and shook it dry out the doors behind him.

"Hello," she greeted.

"Hello," he replied.

"You want a drink?"

His brown eyes fixed on her. "I'm off for the night. Just wanted to be sure you and Nate'll be all right in the storm. I know he don't care for thunder." The hat in his hands spun nervously around, his twitching fingers showing his nerves, and then he ran a hand back through his red hair.

Jasper was crazy about her, all right. To his credit, he rarely hid his interest. Their relationship had become a dance, a daily flirtation or two in passing or during the odd encounter. Just before a storm was not a time for flirtation. Callie had patrons to see to, a saloon to secure before any damage could happen and, if thunder and lightning started, a little boy who was going to need her to rush up the stairs and surround him in comforting cuddles.

"So far he's sleeping. I think he might sleep through it, knock on wood. We'll be fine. You best get yourself home before the rain comes."

"I don't mind a little rain."

He half-smiled at her when he said it. Curses, but his smile was adorable. The last thing she needed was a man appealing to her baser instincts and causing her trouble. "Jasper—"

"I could stick around, if you wanted." He so badly wanted her to tell him to stay. Every muscle on his handsome face tensed with hope.

Men and their trouble. Men and their promises. Callie needed to take care of herself and her son, and hellfire but she meant to do it.

"Go home," she said. "See to yourself."

The words were meant to be final, and he took them that way. He'd barely left when the rain got harder, and she felt the wind pick up. For a moment, she thought about rushing about to call Jasper back—but she didn't follow through.

The first thunder came, and her skin prickled.

Maybe the storm would wash away all her troubles and her memories. Maybe it would wipe the slate clean.

"Mama!"

Her mother's ears picked up the tone of Nate, awake and calling for her.

Or maybe the storm had other plans.

CHAPTER TWO

Jasper

She'd blown him off.

In under a minute of talking, Callie had told him to get lost.

Jasper's heart ached. By God, Callie Lee was going to be the death of him.

Two-and-a-half years had passed since that terrifying day when the madman had come to Cricket Bend and nearly killed Sheriff Anderson and his daughter Haven. Intent on settling an old score in blood, Philip Frank nearly got his wish.

On that day, Jasper had realized he loved Callie Lee.

While a fiery hell was breaking loose a few miles outside of town, the pretty blonde had paced the boardwalk outside the saloon fraught with worry. Jasper had been left behind to watch the town while the sheriff and deputy had gone off, not knowing if they'd be coming back.

Back and forth on the boardwalk outside the saloon, Callie had paced. As she'd mumbled and

11

sworn and tried a few times to grab his gun and go after the lawmen who'd ridden off, Jasper had argued with her, yelled at her a time or two, and realized she was made of more than he'd ever expected and was everything he could ever want.

Those two-and-a-half years felt more like two hundred.

There was no pretty way to say it—she'd worked upstairs at the saloon as a prostitute when he'd met her. Anyone who was going to judge her had best be ready to judge him too. He'd gone to her for the carnal services she offered. He'd paid her for pleasure more than once, and that had been the entirety of their relationship at the time.

Sure he'd been a little sweet on her, but what was not to be sweet on? Lush blonde hair, the prettiest face west of the Mississippi, and a form that could make a man's mouth go dry, all fine packaging for a tough little filly who swore and drank and gave the boys hell when it was necessary.

Callie Lee was his kind of woman right from the start.

But by the time he'd realized he liked her for more than just a quick tumble, she'd been another man's girl. A bounty hunter, Jack Braxton, had come to town and taken all her attention and got her thinking he was going to marry her and raise her baby and everything would be hunky-dory. The man had spun castles for her, and then up and left so no one could tell if he'd meant any of it.

He'd been gone over a year now, vanished like a ghost. Some days it seemed like Callie was mourning him, and others it seemed like she was ready to go chase him down and string him up. She'd had her baby, stopped working in her former profession, and had taken over and run the saloon incredibly well, all while being the sweetest little mother the world had ever seen.

And Jasper found himself falling more and more in love with her every day.

"Jasper!" Darting toward him across the street came Matthew Frank. The rain had already soaked Matthew's golden hair to his head, but he smiled nonetheless. A loud thunder crack cut the air. "Gonna be a big one."

"You heading home?" Jasper asked.

"Should have left an hour ago."

"Haven by herself?"

"Yep," Matthew said. "And smart enough to know to get for the cellar at the first sign of trouble, thank goodness. Still, I'm gonna beat feet. You ridin' for home?"

Jasper looked back toward the saloon. Callie had brushed him off, so there was no reason to go anywhere else but home. "Reckon so."

"All right," Matthew said. "Ride safe, Jasper."

"You too."

They parted ways—Matthew went to his horse, tied not a hundred yards away outside the jail, while Jasper headed to the livery where he boarded his horse during his days in town. Ducking into the stable, he heard the rain start falling. It wouldn't be long before the water came down heavy and relentless.

Dorothy, his mare, stood in her stall.

"Hey girl," he greeted. "You ready to try and

outrun the rain?"

From a beam, he pulled down his saddle and stepped into the stall with Dorothy. The mare was gentle as a lamb, and didn't fight being saddled. Jasper gave her a pat on the rump.

"Jasper," a voice called.

He tried not to sigh too loud.

Ellie Graham had followed him to the barn.

"Hell of a storm coming. You should get home." There was no need to look at her, so he kept to his task.

Slipping into the stall by his side, Ellie wiped a drop of water off her cheek. "I thought you might like to come to dinner at my place." Where she'd placed herself, there was no way he couldn't see her. Standing in the barn in with her mousy brown hair elegantly twisted up and wearing a fancy purple dress with white trimming, she looked ridiculous. Jasper had never understood why a woman who lived in a small Texas town would wear a bustle in the first place, but the kind of women who wore them tended to steer clear of barns. Ellie held up her hem with a disdainful wrinkle of her nose at the dirt floor of the barn. "Doesn't anyone ever clean this place?"

Jasper reached for the bridle. "Come to dinner with you and your husband. Why on Earth would you think that would be fun?"

"Charles is off in Greeley doing business."

Thank goodness he had turned away from her, for he was fairly sure his expression would have revealed his surprise.

Secret meetings with Ellie Graham weren't a

new thing for Jasper. They'd spent most of their teenage years finding places for stolen kisses and rolling around, but it had been a while. That Ellie had married a rich man not two days after she'd turned nineteen years old still stung him.

He'd thought he would marry her, once. He'd been so convinced of it that even her marrying Charles Graham, a banker twenty-five years her senior, hadn't stopped the two of them from meeting. The recklessness of youth, the hot blood of his Irish ancestors, and a good dose of stupidity had kept them at their foolish meetings for longer than was right.

No more. He'd ended it, though she had disagreed loudly.

"That's a bad idea," he replied. "Go home, Ellie." She was silent for a moment, clearly shocked by his refusal. "You're married."

"And that didn't used to bother you. I swear I don't understand you anymore."

"People change."

"Not always for the better, it would seem."

"Dammit, Ellie. Go home."

He turned his back on her, hoping she'd understand he meant it. The retreating sound of her heeled boots clicking on the barn floor answered him. He hadn't meant to be short with her, but she nagged at him.

"Come on, girl," he said to Dorothy as he led her from the barn. Together, they rode swift. The mare didn't seem to mind being asked to run though the rain as it pelted heavier. Jasper tucked his head down, the rain dripping off the brim of his hat and adding to the wetness on the thighs of his pants.

Cricket Bend had been his home his whole life. He'd grown up on a farm just outside the town, gone to school at the small schoolhouse with Matthew and his wife, Haven. He'd fished in the bending creek, raced horses with Matthew across the fields, and eventually fallen into his job as second deputy under Sheriff Luke Anderson.

The man he'd been three years ago and the man he was now were so different he wouldn't have recognized himself. Honestly, he'd been a waste of a young man who'd spent all his money on drinking and women, but then things had changed.

Callie had changed them.

She was no delicate doll. The woman was a fighter, and wise in the ways of the world. To be the kind of man she deserved, he needed to be better. He'd need to be a grown-up instead of a dumb, lazy kid. He was twenty-six now, and she was thirty and a mother and a business owner. In order to match her, he'd have to bring something to the table.

So he'd pulled his life together. He'd stopped sneaking around with Ellie, though she walked around with a snide expression like he'd come to his senses eventually. He'd started to save his pay, and when he'd accumulated enough he bought a little piece of land by the creek and put up a house the past fall. He and Matthew and some others had built it, with some help from folks who'd popped in to assist.

Everyone knew Jasper like everyone knew Callie, and the people of the town were his friends. Cricket Bend was home. He'd come to realize that he could help keep it safe as a lawman. It felt good to have a purpose that meant something.

His house came into sight, and it lightened his heart. He took pride in the house, in the small barn for the horse and short distance to the creek with Pecan trees growing alongside it. In the spring months, the land around his place had been covered with the stunning purple of bluebonnets.

Dorothy rode right into the barn, and Jasper ducked down to get under the door. Inside, he dismounted the horse. He unsaddled and unbridled her. The saddle he hung on a peg on the wall, and he dumped a cup of oats into the trough, threw her some hay, and gave her a few affectionate strokes before sprinting into the house and out of the rain.

He'd bought a length of rope with the plan to put up a tree swing this evening, but thanks to the weather it would have to wait. The swing was for Nate, like the rope and board swing Jasper had spent hours on as a boy growing up not seven miles west of his place.

Jasper had always liked kids, so the addition of little Nate Lee into their lives had been a blessing. The dark-haired boy was a sweetheart with a big smile and now, at nearly three years old, the kind of smarts and personality that led people to say he was precocious. He looked to Jasper as a father of sorts, and Jasper wouldn't let him down. He wouldn't let Callie down, either. A boy needed a father, and Jasper was ready to be that.

Especially since Nate's real father was a good-for-nothing gambler scoundrel who'd nearly torn Cricket Bend apart at the seams before running scared and leaving Callie pregnant and alone.

She'd made the best of it. But, to Jasper's mind, it wasn't enough.

Callie deserved the best, and by god he was going to make sure she got it.

As he'd ridden for home, the thunder had been distant. By the time he reached his door, the noise was ground-shaking and the flashes of lightning illuminated the dim sky. Tree branches moved in the wind.

He wondered if Nate had woken, scared by the storm. If he had, Jasper had no doubt that Callie was right there, holding the boy and calming him.

The wetness of his clothes made them stick to his skin. Jasper took off all his things and hung them on the back of his chairs to dry, then went ahead and got the stove lit. The room warmed quickly.

As the fire heated the iron stove, he went back out onto his small porch.

Jasper had lived all his life in these fields, and aimed to stay.

He didn't, however, aim to be a bachelor like Doc Gray and Hill Hilton.

In the pocket of his drying jacket, there was a little bag, and in the little bag was a ring.

It was for Callie.

CHAPTER THREE

Hank

Most men ran away from trouble.

The smart ones did, at least.

They made a point to go the opposite direction. Onward, never backward. They certainly didn't run toward it, waking up one day with the fool notion to pack all their things, leave a comfortable life in a vibrant city, and get on a train bound back to a dusty little town where nothing but trouble waited for them.

But most men weren't Hank Porter, and most places he'd been in his life hadn't stung him the way Cricket Bend had.

"Tar and feathers," he muttered to himself. Maybe that's how he'd be greeted, with hot tar and chicken feathers thrown at him in the street. Maybe it would be with the click of a pair of handcuffs binding him. Maybe he had a firing squad, or farmers with pitchforks and torches, to look forward to.

Or maybe he was headed right toward one single

bullet fired from the gun of Deputy Matthew Frank with the aim of a man possessed by jealous rage.

Matthew should be jealous and afraid, even after all this time. His wife was one of two things Hank was going back to Cricket Bend for. Sure, Hank was more likely to be greeted by a slap from Haven Frank than a kiss, but it didn't deter him. He could never explain his reasoning, but they boiled down to a simple fact.

He needed to see Haven, almost as much as he needed to see his son.

Thanks to an encounter with his furious ex-wife, Hank knew the boy's name was Nate. Thank goodness for Emma, without whom he would never have even known he was a father. But that was all she had told him, so he had to wonder about everything else. Nate Lee would be over two years old now. Would he look like Callie, all golden hair and dimpled smiles, or would be take after Hank and be broad and dark-haired? Would Callie even let him see the boy, or would she run scared straight out of town the minute he set foot in the city limits?

Hank looked out the window of the coach as it bounced along the worn trail. As he'd come west, the land had flattened. With miles of flat grassland stretching ahead of him, he couldn't help but compare it to New Orleans. Life was quieter out here, and it unnerved him. The whole damn journey unnerved him, start to finish, and now it appeared there'd be a big storm between him and the end of the trip.

Mountains of clouds built off a ways, but the sky was growing darker. The train had been a smoother ride, more luxurious, but to get on the last leg of the journey he'd had two choices: go it solo on horseback, or squeeze into a coach. Hank didn't care to travel by horse. The smelly creatures too often had attitude and dirtied a man's pants.

His only traveling companion on the four days of the coach journey, an older man named O'Brien bound even further west, snored in ragged gasps. The man had blessedly spent much of the journey dozing, and Hank had spent the majority in his head.

A fat money clip peeked out from the lapel of the jacket the man wore, which had fallen open as he'd shifted in his sleep. Hank reached out a quick hand, plucked it, and took out a few bills. The sleeping man, who came from obvious wealth as evidenced by his fine shoes and the tailoring of his clothes, wouldn't miss the money.

Hank slipped the money clip back into the man's jacket and tucked the bills into his own pocket. Even troubled, he could still pull a trick.

He did not feel particularly good about the small victory. He didn't particularly need the money. Taking it was more instinct than necessity.

The mistakes he'd made in his life would fill pages, if he'd been asked to write them down. He'd swindled folks, he'd stolen from folks, he'd used people to obtain the things he'd wanted, and he'd broken the hearts of good women who'd been foolish enough to fall for him. Some of them he barely gave a second thought to, but there were three pangs in his heart he'd never let stop.

Emma, hair red as fire with the voice of an angel,

his former wife. She was married to a cowboy and living on a ranch near Laredo now. It did his heart good to know she was fine and flourishing. Emma came out on top of any situation she was thrust into.

Callie, blonde sugar and spice and his former lover and most profitable working girl. Now the owner of his former saloon, so he'd heard, and the mother of his son. Callie he needed to take care of, to settle and see she would be all right. The woman deserved rubies for all the time she'd spent believing him to be a good sort of man, all evidence to the contrary be damned.

And Haven.

Hank's heart still skipped a beat at the memory of the dark-haired beauty and their stolen kisses two summers earlier. She'd been nearly, so very nearly, his on a night in a red dress in secret. He'd kissed her, he'd tasted her skin, but she'd been too smart and he'd been a damned fool and worked an angle and everything had gone to hell. In the end, Haven had returned to the arms of one of the best men to ever walk the earth.

How Hank hated Matthew Frank, now Haven's husband, even as he admired him. What wasn't there to admire? Matthew had a pure heart, and an innate earnest goodness that shone from a handsome face with bright blue eyes. It was enough to make a jealous man want to vomit.

Cricket Bend was resolution. He'd get there the next day, most likely. They weren't far out from Ridgeville, the nearest town east from Cricket Bend. Hank had hoped to arrive without the delay of another night, but he knew the driver wouldn't risk riding into a storm.

The coach sped up as the raindrops fell faster.

Tomorrow, then.

Tomorrow he would get to Cricket Bend.

Tomorrow he would try to end things, to close the doors he'd left open and wondering when he'd left so quickly two years earlier.

He'd behave himself, or at least appear to.

As long as no one shot him on sight, it might just work.

CHAPTER FOUR

Callie

The storm passed in the night and the street turned to mud. Callie had held tight to Nate the whole night through, letting the boy be soothed by her embrace, though at one point she'd had to sneak downstairs to latch a pair of shutters that had blown open in a gust of wind.

It had not been a restful night, but the smell of the crisp, earthy air after the storm almost made up for it. As the sun came up, Callie brought Nate down to the saloon and settled him at a table with a cup of milk and some bread with apple jelly, and some chalk and a board while she prepared to open up for the day.

He ate mindfully, and scratched lines on the board. A few of them resembled a letter N. In the next year or two or so, he'd be able to start going to the schoolhouse and learning, but she was starting him on his letters and writing early. Maybe he'd grow up and go to college. Maybe he'd become a doctor or a lawyer.

Having a child had changed so many things in Callie's life. Before Nate, the saloon had always been open, but now she closed up around two in the morning and didn't open again until late morning. There'd been some grumbling from a few patrons, but they'd adjusted. She'd had the sheriff's backing, after all, and incidents of late-night drunkenness and mischief were down.

Callie didn't mind the grumbling. She'd have closed the saloon at midnight, or earlier, if there'd been need. Nate, fortunately, could sleep through most anything.

"That one's backwards, sugar." She leaned over his shoulder to tap the board by one of his letters, and kissed his adorable cheek while she was there. He smelled of apples, and his face was sticky. She smiled and wiped him clean.

"Morning, Callie."

"Morning, Ben."

Her bartender, Ben, arrived and headed to the back to bring out new bottles of spirits to replace those that had been consumed the day before. Ben was quiet, bespectacled, but a sweet man. He didn't talk much, but he poured drinks fast, was always on time, and Callie was grateful for him. Hill Hilton arrived first, and settled into a table by the window, another person who was a part of the fabric of the saloon. Ben and Hill together often felt like the support beams that held the place up.

"Mayor Calliope Lee. Oh my stars, that has a nice ring to it."

Before Callie turned around to the door, she knew who had spoken.

Haven Anderson stood in the doorway of the saloon, arms folded over the front of her blue dress.

"Jeepers, word travels fast."

A big smirk sat on Haven's pretty face. "Papa couldn't wait to tell me your plan."

Callie wiped down a table. "Your papa can't keep a secret to save his hide."

"This is a quiet town." Haven shrugged. "Not much else to do but tell secrets. Besides, I don't see why it has to be a secret. I think it's a wonderful idea, and I want to help."

"Good," Callie said. "'Cause I was already planning on your help."

"You need help with something?" Hill asked, having overheard.

Callie turned to him. The news would be leaking out already, no doubt. "I'm gonna run for mayor."

"No kidding!"

"You gonna vote for me?" Callie asked.

"Hell," Hill replied with a big grin. "Can't think of anyone I'd rather vote for. You can count on me, and Ed and Rip too. Better you than Charles Graham. He's got a stick up his—"

"Hill," Haven said his name in a warning tone and cast a glance toward Nate, who sat scribbling on a chalkboard.

Hill covered his mouth. "I'm just saying that a town needs a mayor with some fire in them. You, you got fire. Charles Graham is nothing but blowing smoke."

"Did you file your papers to run?" Haven asked.

Callie nodded to the bar. "Going over to do it shortly."

"If you want, I can get to work making posters. 'Vote for Callie! She'll spit at you if you don't.'" Haven sat at the chair next to Nate's and smiled his way. He held up his chalkboard. "That's good, Nate. I might put you to work on the posters too."

Haven's enthusiasm was honest, but Callie paused.

Haven noticed, of course. "What?'"

Callie stepped closer to her friend, wringing her cloth in her hands. "Are you up for this?"

Haven's smile faded. "I'm fine."

Her best friend on the earth was far from fine. Callie noticed it every day in small things, the darkened purple circles under her big brown eyes, the way she walked slower where before she practically sprinted from place to place, and that it was so early in the morning and Haven was already in town and her husband wasn't by her side.

There'd been a time when Haven and Matthew Frank could hardly pull themselves apart to handle the most important of life's business, they were so caught up in each other, but Haven came to the saloon alone now. She didn't drink, but she was there a lot. She was mourning, same as Callie was.

Hell, but Callie should have told her about Jack. Though she didn't want to add to Haven's sadness. Losing a baby was hard enough.

Haven looked around the saloon for a moment. "I can't sit at home and be sad for the rest of my life," she said. "Doc says I'm fine. I need something to take my mind off things, and this might be just the ticket."

"What does Matthew think?"

"I didn't ask him."

Yet another hint of unhappiness between the Franks. "Are the two of you all right?"

"We're getting by."

Callie's eyes darted to Haven's flat midsection, then away as fast as she could. She didn't believe for a second that Haven and Matthew were fine, but it didn't seem the time or place to push it. "Well, fine then. That's good. Because I don't know how in the hell I can do this without you."

"Matthew'll help with the posters if I tell him to. I'll ask Jasper too."

Callie sighed.

"Oh Lord," Haven said. "What now?"

No one on Earth knew more of Callie's confidences than Haven, and Jasper Tanner was a fairly large part of that. "Can we not ask Jasper?"

Haven sighed. "No one is going to work harder for you."

"But he's going to look at me all…"

"Loving?"

"Yes."

"And what's wrong with that? He's a sweetheart."

"I thought you didn't like him."

"When I was nine, I didn't like him. He was obnoxious, and he followed Ellie around like a puppy and she was even more obnoxious."

"Some things don't change."

"Jasper did. I'll admit, he's grown on me these past few years. Heck, he came out for dinner a few weeks back and even made me laugh a couple times, and that's not the easiest thing to do, I think we can agree on that. You can do worse than Jasper. Much worse."

That was sure true. Of all the men Callie had known in her life, and there had been quite a few, Jasper stood at the top of the heap, a good man with a big heart and an even bigger sense of determination.

How many times had she brushed him off since deciding she needed to make her own way in the world? Several.

How many times had he let her be? None.

Jasper hung around, keeping his distance, but he stayed. He was always where when Callie needed a hand, and had stepped up to be the closest thing to a father Nate had. The boy loved Jasper. And what wasn't to love? And he had that crooked smile that warmed her skin every time he threw it her way, even when she tried her hardest to pretend it didn't. It warmed her, just thinking about it.

"Any word from Braxton?"

The name interrupted her pleasant thoughts of Jasper. She shook her head.

"I bet he's off having the adventure of a lifetime, and thinking of you every second." Even as she said the words, Callie could see Haven didn't mean them. The sweet woman was trying to make Callie feel better, even when she herself was miserable. There was no way Callie could tell her the truth, that Jack was done with adventures and six feet under, knowing it would make Haven even more unhappy.

Tears threatened Callie's eyes. She pulled her hands from Haven's and tapped at the table. "You know, this table is looking dull. I'll go get the polish. I'll be back in just a minute."

She extracted herself to the storage closet in the back behind the bar, and leaned on a shelf of bottles to compose herself. Jack Braxton was long gone, and she had to move on.

"Can you write your name, Nate? N-A-T-E." The sound of Haven's voice, and Nate's in return, made her wipe her eyes clear and take a deep breath.

She could not think about Braxton. No good would come of it, and there was no time to waste on ghosts. Dead or not, he'd been like any other man in the end, spun her head, said he loved her and would marry her even though she was carrying another man's baby, and then turned tail and run for the hills. He'd been gone a long time, and maybe he'd never planned to return at all.

Men were a damn waste of time. All of them. Even Jasper and his smile.

Standing in a supply closet all day dwelling on it was silly. There was a child to be brought up, a saloon to be run, a friend to save from sadness, and a town in need of a mayor with some fire.

The polish. She needed to bring back the polish or Haven would notice she'd been lying to escape the conversation. She stretched up on her toes to reach a container of wood polish, and came back to the ground to realize that the saloon had fallen completely quiet. There wasn't even the sound of Ben rattling bottles. No footsteps could be heard. No glasses scraping along the bar or clinking as Ben stacked them. She didn't hear Nate's little voice, and didn't hear Hill clearing his throat.

Callie stepped out from the storeroom, unsure what she'd find.

"Hello, Callie."

"Sweet Father Christmas," she whispered.

Filling the doorway, Hank Porter held his hat in his hands. Over six feet tall, broad-shouldered and dark-haired as he'd ever been, a handsome devil in the flesh. The astonishment Callie felt at the sight of him was too great, the disbelief all-consuming. It was as if a dead man had risen from the grave. Of all people, he was the one she thought she'd never see again.

Fainting didn't seem out of the question. She could have greeted him sweetly. Instead, she frowned. "What in the hell do you want?"

Hank smiled a bit. "That's about how well I figured this would go."

With sudden realization, Callie found Haven. The brunette appeared to have been shocked right up and out of her seat, staring open-mouthed with a fixed gaze on the sight of Hank in person, and it was no wonder. For all Callie and Hank's past exploits, there was something about Haven and Hank that no one truly understood, probably not even the two of them.

If Callie was shocked to see Hank, Haven would have been nearly struck dead with a heart attack.

Hank tried to keep his focus on Callie and not look at Haven, but she pulled him. His eyes could not stay off her, returned to her.

Haven started to say something, stopped herself, and turned to Callie. "I'll see you later."

31

"You bet," Callie said.

To get out of the saloon, Haven had to pass Hank. She didn't look at him, but kept her head down, but even the closeness when she passed Hank made him close his eyes just for a moment. Callie didn't miss the way he was overcome just being near her.

Then Hank's eyes opened and came to rest on Nate.

Callie's hackles raised. "You," she called to him. "Upstairs, now. Ben, Hill, can you watch Nate?"

Callie took the stairs quickly, and Hank followed right behind. They went to the second floor hallway, and Callie led him to the very end of the hall before going into the last door. Other than a bed and a dresser, the room was vacant. It had been Hank's room once, and the sight of it make him take in a sharp breath.

"You better have a goddamn good reason for showing up here." Callie unleashed a torrent of words at him the second she closed the door. "If you've come to mess with any of us, you're a fool."

"I did not come to mess with anyone."

"Didn't you?"

Hank's back was to her. "I came to see you, and to meet my son."

"You know about Nate."

He chuckled. "When last I faced my former wife, she gave me an earful about what a no-good devil I was. Somewhere in the middle of the names I shall not repeat, she mentioned that I had left you in a motherly way."

"That you did."

"I didn't know."

"Because I didn't tell you I was with child—and until he was born and I saw him, I wasn't even sure he was yours."

"That was him downstairs, then."

"It was."

Hank sighed, a long sound. "He's beautiful."

"He's the moon and the stars. He's the sweetest thing I've ever known. And he is not for you to use in some grand scheme."

"I'm not here for a scheme, I swear." He held up his hands. "You look good, Callie."

"I'd tell you the same, but you already know that."

And damn, but he did look good. It was a great unfair truth of the world that Hank Porter could come through a flood and fire and he'd still be the handsomest man in four territories. No wonder women fell over themselves when he was around. Callie was certain his list of conquests was longer than she would ever know.

"You could have written to me and told me about him."

"I didn't know where to find you. Apparently Haven did. I hear you wrote her letters." That he'd written to Haven after his departure and not to Callie burned a little. They'd been tighter than tight, thick as thieves, but when Hank had left Cricket Bend he'd gone without so much as a farewell. He'd vanished, reappeared to kidnap Haven, and after a night of fire and flames at a burning barn with Luke, Matthew, Braxton, and a madman, Hank had left for real. No one had heard a word from him

33

since, except for letters he'd written to Haven in secret.

"I won't claim I've done things right," he said. "In fact, I'm the first to admit I've done a lot wrong."

"Did you come back to atone?"

"Truth be told, I'm not entirely sure what I'm doing here. I had a delightful setup in New Orleans—a gaming hall, wealthy patrons, all the music I could hear, and the food—" He sighed at the thought. "Incomparable. Only a fool would have left."

Rubbing her hands over her face, Callie groaned. "Your timing, Hank. It's terrible."

"How so?"

"I'm running for mayor."

"Congratulations."

"Your being here is not going to help me. Folks still talk about what happened—that night."

"Would you like me to depart?"

His leaving wasn't what she wanted, not one bit. Having him there felt strange, an odd sort of comfort in a time of many troubles. Hank was far from constant, or reliable, but he was a friend.

"I would like my town and my friends to not be harmed in any way by your being here."

"They won't be."

"I want you to be a model citizen. You will stay at the hotel or boarding house, not here."

"Yes, ma'am."

"And you will keep your distance from Haven."

He didn't agree quickly, so Callie continued talking. "And most importantly, and I am dead serious about this, you will not tell Nate you're his daddy. We're fine, he and I. We have a good life. I won't have him putting his hope on you, and you running off again."

Hank nodded, once. "I understand."

"Do you?"

"Callie…"

"Don't make me regret feeling happy to see you."

When he heard she was happy to see him, Hank smiled. "How is everyone? Haven looked well."

"Hank Porter!" Callie plopped down on the bed, unable to hold back a laugh. "You couldn't even wait thirty seconds!"

"Emma said she was with child."

Giving Hank information about Haven didn't seem right. It wasn't Callie's place to tell what had happened, and she knew it. Yet, if she didn't, Hank was sure to go sniffing around, trying to do whatever it was he aimed to. Maybe, just maybe, if Hank knew what Haven had been though he'd give her space. The two of them had shared something more than passion, in their day. "She was."

Hank had been looking around the room, but stopped. "Was?"

"She was, and then she wasn't." The dimming of his green eyes showed that Hank took her meaning. "It's been almost a year since it happened, and she's just starting to come back to us the way she used to be. Damn, but your timing is terrible."

"How's Matthew?"

"Don't you dare pretend like you care." Callie scoffed.

"I don't hate him."

"He has what you want."

"What I want at this moment is a drink."

"You may have one. You may have as many as you pay for. You are a customer of my saloon, and you'll pay for your drinks and act like any other customer. Once you've drunk your fill, you will go get yourself a room at the hotel or boarding house and act like any other decent person while you are in town."

"Yes, ma'am, Madam Mayor."

"Mayor." That reminded her of the papers she needed to go to the jail and file. Lord, but she was going to have to be the one to tell the sheriff that Hank was back in town. Luke was not going to be pleased.

"I'll be a shining example of a model citizen."

Callie looked at the ceiling and sighed. "I hope you mean that." She went toward the door, and Hank followed her back to the hall and down the stairs. "So you came all the way from New Orleans?"

"I did. Rode out last night's storm at that sham of a hotel in Ridgeville. I'm nearly certain my mattress was stuffed with hay. I spent the better part of the night getting poked."

"I'm not sure our hotel is much better." Nate was sitting at the front table with Hill, and the older man was spinning a coin on the table to the boy's delight. Going around the bar, Callie reached for a glass and poured Hank a whiskey, the drink she'd always known him to prefer.

"That should be your first act as mayor," Hank

said. "If you want people to come visit Cricket Bend, make it a nice place for them. Give them fine accommodations and entertainment. Make them want to stay."

"I already run the best saloon in twenty-five miles."

"Folks who drink need to sleep. I'd think the hotel would be a prime investment."

"Charles Graham owns it."

"The banker?"

Callie nodded. "And my sole competitor for mayor."

"What's he like?"

She shrugged. "He's not the type of man who comes here drinking. I do know he's married to the most vile of women, though. Ellie Graham heads up the Women's Society with her mother. Do you remember George and Laura Harper?"

Hank gave a little wave to Ben. "Good to see you, Ben."

"Hank." Ben looked nervously at Callie for approval. Hank had been his boss once, and Ben had been there for everything that had transpired. The poor man looked back and forth between Hank and Callie like he wasn't sure if he should run off himself.

"Give him what he wants," she said. "But make sure he pays for all of it."

"The Harpers run the general store," Hank said, remembering.

"And a good number of other things," Callie replied.

"So you're going up against a man who runs the

bank, and who has members of family running a good portion of the rest of town."

"Am I insane?"

Hank held up his shot of whiskey. "No, but you're in for a fight."

"That's comforting."

Nate scampered toward Callie, holding the coin in his hand.

"Are you stealing from Mr. Hilton already?" Callie laughed, and reached over the bar to take the coin. "Or is he paying your tab, Hill?"

Hill laughed.

Nate turned his dark eyes to the tall man he stood next to. To look up and see Hank's face, the boy had to tip his head nearly all the way back.

"Nate, honey, this is Hank Porter," Callie said. "He's an old friend of mine."

"Nate," Hank said. "It's nice to meet you."

Nate studied Hank, but didn't say anything. Hank snapped his fingers, reached down, and lifted the boy up to sit on the bar. "Do you like magic, Nate?"

From his pocket, Hank pulled a deck of cards. Sliding her arms around Nate, Callie rested her head on his shoulder to see the trick. After shuffling the cards deftly, Hank held them out to Nate. "Pick one of those, would you?"

Nate picked one card. "Don't show it to me," Hank said.

It was a queen of hearts. Callie put her mouth to Nate's ear. "Remember what's on the card."

"All right, give it back." Nate did, and Hank shuffled it back into the deck. He did a few fancy flourishes as he blended the cards, and Nate watched with great focus. Hank wiggled his fingers over the cards and made a face of hard concentration.

"Wait a second," he said. "This isn't right."

"What isn't?" Callie asked.

Hank opened his eyes and looked into Nate's. "Your card isn't in this deck." He snapped his fingers, and reached behind Nate's ear. "Oh, there it is."

When he withdrew his hand, it held a card.

"That's your card, sugar," Callie said to Nate. "The queen of hearts."

"Just like your mama." Hank winked at Callie.

It was elementary sleight of hand, but to a child Hank had just done real magic. Nate took hold of the card and showed it to Ben, who couldn't hide his smile.

"Wait one more minute," Hank said.

"Oh Lord," Callie whispered.

Hank reached behind Nate's other ear, and came back holding a small toy train.

Nate grabbed it with a giggle.

"Hank!" Callie admonished.

"I have no idea where that came from." Hank shrugged. "When the magic calls me, I am no more than a vessel."

"Mama, a train," Nate said. He kicked excitedly until Hank put him back down on the ground, then ran over to the steps and started to play with the train, making choo-choo noises.

"He's got a book about trains," Callie said.

"Every little boy likes trains," Hank replied with

an easy shrug. "He's a sweet boy."

"He gets it from me," Callie said. Hank raised an eyebrow at her. "I am the sweetest woman in the whole west. Do you disagree?"

"No, ma'am," he said. "I have never seen you drink a man under a table, or throw a man off a balcony. Never in my life."

"Keep it that way," she said.

CHAPTER FIVE

Jasper

Maps of the territory around Cricket Bend covered Matthew's desk.

Two farms to the north of Cricket Bend were squabbling about borders. The Gormans and the Fowlers had been friends for as long as Jasper could remember, but it had all gone to hell recently. A few of their hands had beat the tar out of each other and wound up at Doc Gray's clinic needing stitches and set bones. Luke had gone off early to try and get them to settle it without further violence. This time Matthew had gone with him, and Jasper was running the jail by himself for the day.

If there was going to be a land war, there'd be trouble. Farm boys could fight like nobody's business, and both farms had a number of grown sons to be their soldiers.

Jasper ran a hand through his red hair, noting it had grown longer than he liked, and put his head in his hands to think.

He, Luke, and Matthew would need help. They'd

been able to call on Paul, Jimmy, and Bryce Archer before—three near-identical brothers born one on top of the other, and each keen to be lawmen. He'd ask Luke about letting them know the situation, in case they were needed. More men might be able to break up an all-out fight between all the men of the squabbling lands, but the farms were four miles to the north of town, and if trouble broke out, it could be over and done with casualties before they reached the farm border.

They could station a man there to watch over things. They could stop by a few times a day, or put out a call for a few extra men to be ready to ride out in case of trouble, but nothing they could likely do would be enough to hold down two ranches full of men with blood on their minds.

Solving the problem outright would be best, but how to do it?

Sighing deep, Jasper leaned forward and put his head on his arms to rest for a moment.

Cricket Bend needed to grow up, the same way he'd had to. Clear the hurdle of being a dusty little town with rough edges and grow into something more. With the pretty location on the creek and the good soil, the town could grow into something truly special.

On the table in the pile of papers, he saw Charles Graham's application for mayor. Electing a mayor seemed a good first step toward the future the town could have, though Jasper had his own reasons for disliking Charles Graham that had nothing to do with the man's personality. It was hardly the banker's fault that Ellie had chosen him over Jasper, though he tried not to roll his eyes at every mention of Charles Graham.

There was a knock on the door.

Jasper raised his head. Like an angel sent to relieve his troubles, Callie stood there. Even in a brown dress, high-collared and prim, she was pretty as a wildflower.

"If you need a drink, I know where you can get one."

"At this rate, I might need the whole bottle."

"Bad day?"

"It's a little better," he said. "At least you ain't a farmer."

Callie knew all about it. "The boys still riled up?"

"Yep. Luke and Matthew went out again to try and settle it."

"Poor Luke," Callie said. "Like he doesn't have enough to work on."

"What brings you to the jail this fine morning, Miss Lee?"

She held out a folded paper. "I need to file my papers. I'm going to run for mayor." When Jasper grinned, she pulled back her hand a bit. "It's a damned crazy notion, I know. You think I'm loopy, don't you?"

"Nope. I think it's the best idea I've ever heard."

"You teasin' me?"

"Hell no. I think you'd make a fine mayor."

Callie sighed. "Let's hope the rest of the town feels the same."

Jasper held out his hand to take the papers. "Luke ain't likely to be back for a while, most likely. I can take your papers and see he gets them."

"I would appreciate it." She handed them over, and stepped back to the door. "Thank you."

"Charles Graham is running for mayor."

"I know. Anyone else running?"

"Not that I know of."

Callie nodded, but her mind was elsewhere.

"Everything all right?"

Callie had started to leave, but stopped in the doorway. Something was up with her, had her tighter-wound than normal. "I don't know," she confessed.

The notion that she might be in some trouble twisted around in his gut. When Jasper spoke again, it was quieter so as to not scare her. "You ever gonna not run away from me?" Callie started to protest. "Come on, Callie. We been through enough we should at least be able to talk to each other. You're sore at me for something, tell me. Else I'm likely to second-guess everything I ever done."

"I am not sore at you," she said.

"Bull," he answered.

"I'm not!"

"You blew me off last night, and you're barely looking at me right now."

"You needed to get home and not stand in a thunderstorm." He would have done just that, to be honest. Rain, thunder, wind, he wouldn't have felt a bit of it. "Besides, right now I have other things on my mind."

"Like what?"

"Hank Porter is sitting in my goddamn saloon." Finally, the truth.

44

Jasper froze. "You're telling tales."

"I am not," she said. "He walked in an hour ago lookin' the same as the day he left."

Matthew and Luke weren't in town. They wouldn't have known, and if anyone needed to know it was them. Jasper stood up and came around the desk until he was close to her. No one was around, but he dropped his voice anyway. "Who all knows?"

"Anyone who saw him get off the morning coach, I imagine. Plus Ben, Hill, and Haven were with me when he showed up."

"Callie—"

His eyes got wide. Callie held up a hand. "You don't have to tell me how dangerous this is."

Dangerous was an apt word. Hank Porter was like a spark too close to a powder keg, and one wrong move could start something terrible all over again. "What are you going to do?"

"What can I do?"

"Ask me to shoot him." He said it in all seriousness, but it was a tease.

Callie got it. Both of their expressions turned to smiles.

"You'd do that for me."

"Hell yes. I'd do anything for you." Callie blushed. The sight of it gave him a sense of triumph. "I wish you wouldn't push me away all the time."

"If it helps, it is getting harder and harder to. You sure don't make things easy."

"How do I make things hard?"

"You could stop being so damned appealing,"

45

she said. "It's real hard to pretend you don't exist when you smile at me like that."

"Like what?" he said with a bigger, more teasing smile.

"Stop it," she said, swatting him. "Things are hard enough as they are."

"I ain't trying to make hard times," he said. "I'm just trying to be a friend to you."

"A friend?"

He shrugged. "A friend would try and help."

"The most helpful thing you could do is go away."

It hurt to hear her say it, but Jasper persevered. "You don't mean that for a second."

"I'm trying to convince myself. Men are more trouble than they're worth, and I do not need another one in my life complicating things. I've already got a six-foot something pile of complicated handsome sitting in my bar. I don't need a good-looking deputy to deal with too."

He grinned. "You think I'm good-looking?"

His answer was a swat to his arm.

"You're set on that, then? That you don't want nothing to do with men."

"I am. And don't you go trying to change my mind."

Jasper feigned offense. "Why, Miss Lee, I wouldn't dare."

She turned and went to the door of the jail. "Make sure Luke gets those. Haven's all set to make posters for me, and I don't want to waste her time."

"What about Hank?"

"I told him to keep his distance. This is a free town, and he has as much right to be here as anyone."

"Is he going to stay at the saloon?"

"He'll take a room somewhere."

"I'll do my best to keep Matthew from killing him."

"And I'll do my best to keep him away from Haven."

Jasper's heart twisted. Since the day he'd met Nate as a baby, he'd wanted to be the boy's daddy. He'd seen him every day, played with him, changed his nappies, and loved the boy. Yet Hank was Nate's father, and that truth was inescapable. "What about Nate?"

Callie shook her head. "I will not have him hurting my son with false hope. That's Hank's calling card, promises and dreams that don't amount to nothing. I will not keep Nate from him, but just because he's the boy's father doesn't mean he gets to be his daddy."

Jasper swallowed hard. "I put up a swing at my place this morning. Thought Nate might like it next time he comes out to go fishing."

Her whole face softened. "He asked me yesterday—*go fishy, Mama.*"

"I'm off after around three tomorrow," Jasper said. "I'll take him out for a bit. I don't mind."

"I know you don't," she said. "He would love it."

"You can come too, if you like." Nate had been out to his place a few times, had fished in the creek and played in the field and ridden Dorothy, but

Callie hadn't yet been out. Would this be the time she'd come out, see his place, and perhaps realize how serious he was in his affections?

"I'll let you two have your time." She smiled. "A boy needs a—"

Father. She'd been about to say father, or Daddy, or Papa, before she blushed red and fled out the door.

A boy did need a father, and Callie needed someone to love her the way Jasper did.

"Why don't you come out?" he asked. "We'll have a campaign meeting—dinner! I'll ask Haven and Matthew to come too." As he spoke, the idea grew in his mind. She'd come out to his place, see how nice it was, and realize how nice the three of them as a family could be.

"Tomorrow?"

He nodded. "Tomorrow it is."

Callie shook her head and smiled at him. "What on Earth am I going to do with you, Jasper?"

"Whyn't you find out?"

He leaned on the doorframe as she left, watching her until she was back in the saloon. With a long sigh, he realized he'd just invited her for dinner the next night.

And there were bigger problems too.

Hank Porter was back.

Two hours passed before Luke and Matthew returned to the jail. Two hours Jasper spent peering out the window at every footstep on the boardwalk and pacing the jail trying to figure out how to say what he had to say, save for fifteen minutes where he helped Delia Lance shoo a stray cat out of the kitchen of her restaurant.

"You settle it?"

Luke fell into his chair. "Nope. Damned farmers. Here I thought cowboys were trouble."

"It's a matter of fifty feet," Matthew said. "And every man involved is more stubborn than a damned mule."

"Anything happen while I was gone?"

Jasper gulped. For two hours he'd been stewing in the news of Porter's return and feeling the heat grow. He did not want to have to be the one to tell them, but it was better it come from him and not a sudden encounter on the street. At least here, in the jail, if Matthew went into a murderous rage, Jasper could probably fight him and lock him in a cell until he cooled down. His mind leapt to all the worst-case scenarios he was about to trigger.

"Jasper?" Luke asked.

Jasper nodded. "Uh, well, you see…"

"Spit it out, son."

"It's kind of funny, really."

"For heaven's sake, just say it," Matthew said. He didn't look at all concerned.

"I'm getting to it."

"Jasper," Luke warned.

"Hank Porter is back."

Luke blinked. "What did you say?"

"Callie came by to file her papers to run for mayor," Jasper grabbed the papers off the desk and thrust them at Luke, as if they could distract from the blow-out that was about to happen. "She said he showed up on the sunrise coach from Ridgeville."

"Where is he?" Matthew asked. He was behind

Jasper, and his tone didn't sound at all like the Matthew Jasper had known all his life. There was ice in his voice, and hatred.

Jasper shrugged. "I don't...that is..."

The next thing he knew he was following the other men out of the jail and over to the saloon. Inside, there was only Ben, Hill, Rip Peters, Callie, and Nate playing with a toy train on the bottom step to the upstairs rooms.

"Callie," Luke called out and waved her over as he walked in. Jasper watched her expression change from peaceful to alert at the sight of them. She clearly knew why they were there, and put on her prettiest hostess smile. "I don't suppose you gentlemen have come to drink on the job."

"Where's Porter?"

"Either gettin' cleaned up at the bathhouse, getting a meal at the restaurant, or getting himself a room at the hotel or boarding house. I ain't his keeper, Sheriff. Thank goodness."

Luke was silent a long moment, his posture tall and his face tense.

Callie took a step closer. "Don't think I don't understand how you feel, Sheriff."

"Has he come to make trouble?"

"He says no."

"Do you believe him?"

"I don't tend to believe many things men say." Callie shot Jasper a look, as if regretting what she said. Her damned stubborn distrust of men, always foremost in her mind guiding all her decisions.

Matthew snorted. "Can't say I blame you."

If Luke's nerves were manifesting in rigid calm,

Matthew looked ready to jump out of his skin. He fidgeted, picking at his fingernails, and he looked around the room as if Porter was going to come jumping out from behind a table with guns blazing.

Matthew and Hank being in the same town likely meant there'd be trouble. Though Matthew was strong and a good fighter, Hank was the kind of man who'd be ruthless in a brawl, who'd fight to win even if it meant killing the other person. If he wasn't, he'd likely have been killed long ago. The world didn't take kindly to scoundrels and cheats.

Callie noted Matthew's discomfort. "You want a drink, Deputy?"

"I don't think that's wise," Matthew answered. "But thank you for the offer. I'd rather be clear-headed right now."

"In case of a fight."

Matthew nodded to Callie. "In case of a fight. 'Cause there's like to be one."

"I have no doubt. If it could happen outside my establishment, I'd be grateful."

"Gentlemen!"

The greeting, lined with the edge of a southern drawl, made Jasper's stomach turn.

Hank Porter walked into the saloon and right up to the conversation. "I can only presume this kerfuffle is in regards to me. Sheriff Anderson, Deputies, I must say I'm flattered." He talked as if he weren't bothered, but Jasper saw him shove his hands in his pockets. Something in Hank's manner showed nerves this time around. Never could Jasper remember seeing the man ever flustered by anything before.

Luke wasted no time. "What's your business in town, Porter?"

"My my, but the welcome wagon around these parts has really fallen to hell since I last arrived in town."

"Look how well that turned out for all of us," Matthew said.

"It seems to have turned out fine for you."

The men stared at each other. Callie came around the bar and stood just to the side of them all.

"Can't a man visit old friends?" A cocky twinkle in his eye, Hank leaned against the bar.

"We should arrest you right now," Matthew growled.

"For visiting a saloon?" Hank answered. He looked around the room to Rip and Ed. "Your jail would be full awful fast if that became a crime. I daresay those two hooligans would take up residence."

"Kidnapping, for starters—" Matthew stepped toward Hank, but Luke held out a hand and stopped him from going any farther.

"And then saving the life of the person he kidnapped," Callie said as she closed the space between Hank and the lawmen. "Boys, I will not defend Hank too often in this life, but I think you should all be able to forgive that. Without him, I hear tell the two of you might not be standing here today."

"Why thank you," Hank said.

She held up a finger to him. "Don't push me. There's lots of things I can't forgive."

Matthew tilted his head. "What about leavin' you

high and dry?"

Callie's eyes flicked over to where Nate played, happily rolling his train over the step. Mentioning him, even in a subtle way, wasn't going to win Matthew her good graces. Her back stiffened. "While I appreciate your concern, Deputy, men do that to women all the time. I don't see the rest of them getting arrested for it."

Luke folded his arms. This was his town, and his daughter was likely the prime reason Hank had come back, but Luke wasn't losing his composure. Above all things, he was a fair man. "One step out of line, Porter. Take one step and see what happens."

It wasn't a challenge. It was a promise.

"Sheriff, I am happy to comply with all the laws of this town during my stay."

"What about the laws of decency?" Matthew asked.

Hank chuckled. "I will attempt to remember those exist as well."

"I'll vouch for him," Callie blurted.

"Callie," Hank started to protest. The idea was crazy even to him, apparently.

"I will. He will be no more harm than a kitten while he's in town. You have my word."

Bullets practically flew from her eyes to Hank, but to the scoundrel's credit he didn't argue. "You heard the lady, Sheriff. No more harm than a kitten."

Luke did his best to keep a straight expression, but Jasper saw the way his fingers tightened around the handle of his gun and the look of displeasure he gave Callie before he left the saloon. Matthew followed right behind, and Jasper had no doubt he was going to immediately find Haven. That was a discussion he was glad he wouldn't be around for.

Hank turned back to the bar and signaled Ben for a drink.

Jasper pulled Callie aside by the elbow.

"I wish you hadn't done that," Jasper said quietly to her.

"Matthew looked ready to kill him."

"Well, maybe he's not wrong. Matthew and Hank, they got bad blood and it's going to eventually have to resolve itself. You might not be able to step between them when it happens. I don't want to see you hurt and I can't always be there to protect you."

"Protecting me ain't your job," she said. "This town is bigger than me."

"Not to me it ain't."

He still held on to her arm. Callie pulled herself free. "Well, then maybe you need to rethink your priorities."

"Tarnation," Jasper whispered.

Callie turned her back on him and went over to Nate. She'd ended the conversation. There'd be no more reasoning with her today. Tomorrow, though, she'd come to his place and...maybe the fates would be on his side.

As he walked from the saloon, he heard Callie's voice. "I swear to God, Hank, if you make one move—"

He smirked a bit. Surely Hank wouldn't be dumb enough to go against Callie. Surely he had at least

54

that much decency in him.

CHAPTER SIX

Callie

Neither Haven nor Callie were much for drawing, but Hill Hilton could wield a pencil pretty well, so the three of them sat around a table in the saloon covered in pieces of paper. With papers filed, now the work of running for mayor truly began.

"Now, I've prepared a list of things to put on the posters. Would you like to hear them?" Haven pulled a folded piece of paper from her pocket.

"Of course."

Haven cleared her throat dramatically. "'Vote for Callie. Why the hell not?'"

Hill whooped. "There you go."

"'Vote for Callie. She'll whoop you if you don't.' 'Vote for Callie. Graham is a weasel.'"

"Aww." Callie giggled. "He is not."

"I know." Haven smiled. "'Vote for Callie. You'd be a fool not to.'"

"Hear, hear!" Hill raised his beer.

"A vote for Callie is a vote for new beginnings." Everyone stopped and turned to the voice who had spoken, cutting into the silly revelry. Hank had slunk in and was watching and listening from the bar. "Play up the fact that you changed your life completely. Folks like a redemption story."

"Hank—" Callie said.

Haven interrupted her. "That's not a bad idea." Haven took the pencil from Hill and started to scribble. "No doubt Charles is going to run on the angle that he has money and connections that can make things happen. You can't beat him that way, but your story is better. Folks do love a redemption story."

"I think we know what the town thinks of my story."

"Not all of them," Haven said. "Lizzie says there's a bunch of the Women's Society who are sick to death of being bossed around. They're all wives and mothers. They might relate to you."

"I doubt they'll want to try."

Callie had faced the Cricket Bend Women's Society before. She'd gone to a meeting thinking they might accept her, but instead she'd gone toe to toe with Ellie and her mother and taken off. Haven had followed her, and from that moment they'd been friends.

Hank stood up. "There's apt to be plenty of people who can't overlook your former profession, and there's nothing you can do about it. Blast them all. They're not the ones you want. You want the regular people, the ones who don't have Graham and Harper money, the ones who've actually had to worry about getting by."

"You planning to run my campaign?"

Hank smiled. "I just want to see you win."

"Why?"

"Because this town needs someone like you to steer it."

The words were touching, even if she questioned his motives. "So what do we put on the posters?"

"Keep them simple," he said. "Let your speech and your interactions show your platform. You're good with people. Get up and tell them your plans."

"When are the speeches?" Haven asked.

"Next Tuesday." Callie looked to Hank. "Will you write my speech for me? I can't imagine anyone around here is better with words than you are."

He smiled. If Hank was playing an angle, she couldn't yet see it. The best she could tell, he appeared genuinely interested. The idea that he might want to position her as mayor in order to get or take something crossed her mind, but she couldn't worry about that yet.

First, she had to win the position. Then she could start playing politics. Right now she needed every ally she could get.

Hill held up a piece of paper on which he'd drawn a rough sketch of a simple sign. **'VOTE CALLIE,'** it said in block letters.

"'Vote Callie,'" she read. "Oh Lord, I'm really doing this."

Haven studied the image before standing up. "I'll get the supplies. Doc needs me back anyway." She put a hand on Hill's shoulder. "Nice work, Hill."

She looked to each of them as she left, pausing a minute at Hank. "You too, Hank."

The simple act of her speaking to Hank seemed enough to knock him out. The man, giant and strong, nearly fainted at finding her words aimed at him. He stammered for a moment as she passed out the saloon doors back to the street, and didn't find his voice until after she was too far to hear.

"Thank you."

Callie gave a little snort.

He met Callie's eyes. "What? I'm behaving myself. I'm taking an interest in local politics."

Callie rose from the table and walked closer to him. "What's in it for you if I win?"

"I'll know Cricket Bend is in the hands of someone who gives a damn."

"Do you give a damn?"

"Of course I do," he said quietly. "This town is full of people I care about. I want to make sure it flourishes."

"You're not being all noble just to impress Haven, are you?"

He shrugged. "If that happens to be the result, then so be it."

Callie rolled her eyes. Hank would be Hank until the clouds fell from the sky and the earth ended. When he wanted something, he was used to getting it. She'd have to keep an eye on him when it came to Haven.

"Where is your darling boy on this pleasant afternoon?"

"Fishing," Callie answered. "Jasper takes him out by the creek."

"Do they ever catch anything?"
"Usually about four or five pounds of mud."

CHAPTER SEVEN

Jasper

When Nate had indicated he wanted to go fishing, what the boy actually meant was that he wanted to poke at the sand and mud at the side of the creek bed, but Jasper didn't mind. He'd been a boy himself, after all, and knew the wonders of a running creek and mud and worms. There was nothing better on a warm fall day.

The plan for the evening's dinner meeting had come together easily. Haven had jumped on the idea, taking over the cooking of dinner, and Jasper was grateful. He could make a few dishes, but nothing as impressive and delicious as what she could come up with. He left the jail around three, grabbed Nate, and headed out for some fishing before readying for the evening. On the way out of town, Matthew had joined up with them.

Now Jasper sat back on the ground against a tree while Nate dangled the string into the water. The boy wouldn't catch much, and was happier to wade to his knees in the water anyway. Matthew sat on a rock and fished, looking seriously at the water. They weren't even a quarter-mile from Jasper's house. He could see the barn up on the hill, in fact.

Nate's hands were covered in mud. He held his grubby fingers up and giggled.

"He's a good kid." Matthew chuckled.

"The best," Jasper replied.

"Shame his father is the biggest son of a—"

"Matthew."

The man looked admonished. "You know what I was going to say."

"Yep. And you ain't wrong. I'm no happier Porter is here than you are."

"I can't believe he got up the nerve to come back."

Jasper waded carefully into the subject. "How's Haven doing with it?"

Matthew glanced down at the earth for a moment. "I'm sure she and Luke had words."

"Didn't you and she have words?"

"She and I—we're having a tough time of things."

Jasper didn't press for more. He'd been there for every day of Matthew and Haven's happiness, the wedding and the honeymoon where they'd gone off to Philadelphia so Haven could train in nursing legitimately, then their return and their readying for the baby, and then for the way they'd crumbled in the aftermath. "Anything I can do to help?"

"You can let me talk about anything else."

Matthew was not a man who shared his feelings easily. He'd never even been someone who talked a lot, but he and Jasper had always been friends for some reason. Since they'd been boys together, they'd been close.

"What do you think is going on with the farmers?"

"Something, that's for sure." Matthew said. "Luke thinks we're not being told something. It just don't make sense. That little piece of land wouldn't grow a potato. Something else is driving a wedge between the two groups."

"They best figure it out soon. Luke seems ready to arrest the whole lot of them."

"It might come to that."

Jasper stretched out his legs and looked up to the blue cloudless sky, deliberately not thinking about the size of the Cricket Bend jail and how it couldn't possibly hold all those men. The fall day was warm, though the air held the slight nip of a hint that autumn was coming. Cricket Bend was blessed with pleasant enough temperatures year round, but on fall and winter nights it got downright cold. He'd need to start chopping some wood and stocking it in the next couple weeks, and should probably get another bag or two of oats to keep around for Dorothy just in case. He could order them from the general store, though that would mean talking to either Ellie's ma or pa.

Ellie wasn't the woman he wanted to think about anymore. Her familiar features melted into Callie's pretty eyes in the picture in his head, and he smiled. "Callie is running for mayor."

Matthew whistled low. "I bet the Women's Society will hate that."

"I bet."

"Ellie know yet?"

"Nope. And I think I'll dig myself a damn hole and hide on the day she finds out. Might stay there until the whole thing passes and the election is done. Though that wouldn't do much good."

"Ellie's bound to hear you had Callie out to your place for a meeting."

"Ellie hears everything."

"The two of you still…?"

"No," Jasper insisted.

"Really?"

"She and I haven't been like that for a while."

"Because you're head over heels for Callie?"

Everyone knew. Not that Jasper had hid his feelings, but to think that everyone in town knew his business was slightly aggravating. "All I want is to be with her."

"There's girls over in Greeley for that."

He was referring to the gaming hall in the neighboring town, not only a saloon but an establishment frequented by gamblers and promising all kinds of sordid delights. Feeling his defenses rise, Jasper sat up. "That ain't what I mean."

"Ain't it?"

"Well, it ain't all I mean. I love her, Matthew."

Matthew turned his head and looked straight at Jasper. "You told her that?"

"Nope."

"Then tell her."

"I can't just—"

"Trust me when I say this. I am no expert on

women by any means. I barely understand my own wife a good deal of the time. But I know this: women need to hear the words. Tell her. Say it loud and clear and hope she hears you."

Nate tripped and fell to his knees in the shallow water. Jasper tensed, not sure if the kid was hurt. But after just a second, Nate started playing in the mud. Kids were resilient, thank goodness.

"Did you always know you wanted to be a husband?"

"Nope. I just knew I wanted Haven."

"You worried about Porter?"

Matthew nodded, his eyes narrowing. There were so many rumors about the events of two summers prior, and what exactly had transpired between Haven and Hank Porter, Jasper wasn't sure what to believe. But he knew that, from it all, had come Haven and Matthew's wedding and the solidarity of the love the two of them had danced around from the time they were all kids.

Matthew took a moment before speaking. "When the devil arrives on your doorstep, you worry. You might want to worry too. He and Callie go back a long way and…" Matthew's eyes set on Nate. "…they got history."

Jasper knew Matthew wasn't wrong. What Hank and Callie had been, besides employer and employee, he'd never been totally sure, but he'd have been a stupid man not to assume two such people wouldn't have had something along the way. She'd come with Hank to Cricket Bend, and left behind Fort Worth. There had to be a big reason for that.

"What would you do if you were me?"

"Ask her out to dinner," Matthew said.

"I asked her out here for dinner."

"Oh, Jasper."

"What?"

"Treat her like a lady. Court her. Ask her to have dinner with you. Get dressed up a bit and take her out on the town. Show her you're not afraid to be seen with her, that you're proud of her. Show the whole damned town that Callie Lee is the girl for you."

"You know, that's not a terrible idea."

"Sometimes I'm worth my keep."

"Matthew?"

"Yeah?"

"Take your own advice."

"I just might," Matthew said. He threw his fishing line back into the creek. "This is nice. I ain't been fishing in a long while. Who knows? Maybe it'll be the last time I ever get to, considering we're likely to get killed by the Fowler boys tomorrow bright and early, at that meeting Luke set up."

Nate came running toward Jasper then, covered in mud and delighted about it. Jasper picked him up and held him out before the mud could get all over his own clothes. "Well, before we die grisly deaths, you want to help me wash this little bug clean?"

"Strip him down and dunk him?" Matthew asked.

Jasper nodded. Nate giggled and touched Jasper's nose with a muddy finger, leaving a smudge.

CHAPTER EIGHT

Callie

Lovely.

That was the only word she could think of to describe Jasper's place. If Callie had ever dreamed up the kind of home she'd like to live in, it would be just the same. Not big or fancy, but well-built and cozy, with two bedrooms and a porch. Her heart yearned for a porch of her own. Jasper had decorated his home simply, with clean white curtains in the windows and a handmade quilt on both beds in the two rooms. It was both a man's home, and a home awaiting a woman's touch.

Callie rode out with Doc Gray, in his wagon. The town doctor was a kind man, and often had keen insight into the ways of Cricket Bend, having lived there for nearly thirty years and having seen it grow from a collection of cattle ranches to a town in the first place. He'd chattered her ear nearly off on the ride out, and she'd talked right back.

By the time she and Doc rode up in Doc's

wagon, Matthew and Jasper were pushing Nate on a rope swing and Haven was hard at work in the kitchen, making the whole house smell like heaven. The gathering before dinner was lively and fun, filled to the brim with activity and chatter, and after being in it for a while, Callie realized she hadn't been so happy in a long time.

For a moment, she pretended the place was hers, that the pots and pans hung on the wall by the stove were hers, and the pretty view that looked down the hill and over the creek was hers, and the pretending was nice.

"But how do we get folks to vote for you?"

The meeting came to order around Jasper's dinner table, as Haven set the last of the dishes she'd cooked out for consumption. The woman could cook like no one's business. She'd made her famous chicken and dumplings and cornbread for the evening, and the room smelled as good as any restaurant.

"You could go to the Women's Society meeting," Matthew suggested.

"Ellie wouldn't let me in the front door."

"Kick it down, then."

"She'd have me arrested."

"Might be the lawmen would look the other way."

"Lots of them have had it with her, you know," Haven said. "Lizzie told me she stopped going to the meetings because she got tired of Ellie thinking she could tell them all what to do."

"There's still a whole lot of them," Doc said. "People's judgment—that's bound to be your

68

biggest challenge."

"Things change," Haven said. "People change too." Just then, Jasper returned from fetching wood for the fireplace. Haven smiled and winked at Callie. "Yes, sir. People change all the damn time."

Nate came in with Jasper, carrying his own log.

For all the times Nate had been out to Jasper's place, Callie had never made the trip. She'd never thought there would be a reason to. A city girl, after all, would never be interested in a quaint cabin in the hills. Yet there she was, charmed by every bit of it.

The men put the wood by the fire before taking their places at the table.

"How's your speech going?" Doc asked. "I hear tell Hank is aiding you with it."

"Yep," Callie said.

"I think it's a fine idea. The man is gifted with words."

Matthew started to say something, no doubt planning to fire an insult, but Callie jumped in before he could. "There's going to be a profile in the paper about me, and one about Charles as well. Teddy Knight is a friend of both the Harpers and Grahams, so I don't know what he'll ask me. I don't want to get all flustered and say something stupid he can blast all over the front page."

"How 'bout I ask you questions?" Doc said.

"How 'bout I try and answer them?"

"That'd be as good a start as any."

"Shoot." She wiped her mouth and sat upright, paying attention. Matthew, Haven, and Jasper listened. Nate munched on the sweet cornbread and crumbs fell on his shirt.

"To begin, Miss Lee, why on Earth would you want to be mayor?" Doc asked.

"I love this town. I aim to use the position to help Cricket Bend grow and to become an even better place for people to live and raise their children."

"Isn't it a fine place already?"

"It is," she answered. "But there's room for improvement."

"Such as?"

"There's never enough money for the schoolhouse. And, right now, folks don't have much of a say in the rules and laws around here, unless they're wealthy."

"Why should folks vote for you and not Graham?"

"Because I know what it's like to have to work hard to get by, like most folks around here. I know what it's like to worry about where your meal is going to come from." A bit of a lump rose in her throat as she spoke. "I'd like to help make it so people don't have to worry about that, and can do more productive things."

Doc held up a hand. "That's all well and good, but I'm gonna ask this next question because Ellie or one of her hens is bound to throw is at you."

Callie anticipated what it would be. "As far as my former profession—yes, I worked upstairs at Porter's saloon. I wasn't born into a rich family, and I left home early and did what I did to get by. I know there are people who don't like me for it, and I can't help that, but I also know firsthand that we shouldn't judge people by their pasts if they're trying their hardest to change. People make mistakes and take wrong paths all the time. We need to be able to forgive."

No one said a word. Four pairs of eyes stared at her.

"Is that good enough?"

"More than good enough," Doc said.

Breathing out, Callie felt flushed suddenly. She bent over her food and stuck a fork in a dumpling. "Would you vote for me, Doc?"

"Damn right I will."

"Me too," Matthew said.

"And me," Jasper jumped in.

"I wish I could vote for you," Haven said.

"I wish I could vote for myself," Callie replied. The sad truth of the matter was that, though a woman could run for the office, she couldn't vote for who would hold it.

"The world will catch up one day," Doc said. "It's trying to."

They strategized and talked until every bit of the food on the table was gone. Nate was excused from the table and went to lay on the rug in front of the fire to play with a few toy wooden horses Jasper kept for him, as well as the toy train he wouldn't let out of his sight. Eventually, Doc excused himself and went to play with Nate, and Matthew joined as well. Haven began to clear the table.

"Let me help you clean up," Callie offered.

Matthew leapt up and went to his wife's side, taking the empty platter from her hands. "Naw, I'll help. You haven't been out here before. Jasper should give you the grand tour."

Callie looked across the table at Jasper, who looked surprised. These clever friends of hers were setting them up, and she knew it. They all knew she knew it.

But it had been such a nice night, and Callie didn't want it to end already. So she nodded in agreement, and gave Haven a look before Jasper led her outside to the porch.

Under the clear sky and in the crisp air, the view from his porch was beautiful.

"Your place is real nice," she said.

"Thank you."

"I like this porch," she said. "I always wanted a porch."

"My folks' place had a porch, and my sister and I used to play on it for hours. So when I decided to build this place, I knew I wanted a porch."

"Where does your sister live now?"

"Kansas," he said. "She's married, and has three kids. All boys under the age of eight."

"Goodness," Callie said. "She must be a patient woman."

"That she is," he said.

"Kansas is a long way," she answered.

"Yep," he said. "Thank goodness the Missouri-Kansas-Texas Railroad opened up. I can get on in Dallas and it takes weeks off the trip. Ma went up there to live with Grace and her family after Pa died about six years back."

"You didn't go with them?"

"I like it here," he said. "Cricket Bend has been my home all my life."

"It's a fine place."

"I got it in my head that I would stay and become my own man. Of course, I wasted a few years being reckless and stupid first."

"I'm not apt to judge for you being reckless and stupid," she said. Jasper laughed a bit. "Though I do recall a young man who fancied himself a scoundrel in training…"

"All that didn't make me happy," he said. "I needed a place to hang my hat, and I needed a porch on which to drink my coffee before I start my day."

"That'd be nice," Callie said wistfully.

"Whyn't you find out?"

Callie laughed. "Jasper Tanner, what on Earth am I going to do with you?"

"Kiss me?"

Her smile ceased. Her throat went dry. "They're right inside."

He crossed the distance between them, taking himself out of the light cast from the lamps inside the house and away from the door. "No one in there would be surprised to see us kissin'."

Callie saw it coming. He ducked down to kiss her. Before his lips met hers, Callie put her hands on his chest and pushed a little to keep distance between them. "No." She turned her head away.

She saw immediately that she'd cut him, deep. "I don't get it," he said quietly. "Not one bit."

"I don't kiss," she whispered to him. She took hold of his collar.

"What?"

"Not unless I really and truly mean it. Call it my moral code, if you want."

"And you don't mean it with me?"

Callie tilted her head up to him. "I'm scared that I do." She swatted him. "Jeepers, you sure don't make things easy on a woman trying to decide things."

"What is there to decide?" he asked. "I know you're still waiting on Braxton—"

A punch to her heart, and she closed her eyes and shook her head. "I'm not waiting on him."

"Then why not be with me?"

He had a point. A damn good one, built on reason and love and all sorts of good things regular people could make decisions based on. And looking at him in the shadows of the porch, the way the dim light kissed his jawline, the way the day's stubble had come in, made her feel all sorts of things that went against her loud-spoken beliefs.

"I…"

"Come to dinner with me," he said. "Tomorrow night. I'll take you out."

"You'd be seen with me?"

"I'd be proud to."

If it were possible for a heart to bloom, hers did. "Come here," she whispered.

He did as he was bid, stepping so close to her their two bodies touched.

"One kiss," she said. "To thank you for arranging this evening. But just one."

"Just one'll be enough."

"No it won't," she whispered.

"I know. I was trying to be chivalrous."

Jasper rested a hand on her waist and used his other hand to cup her chin. If he only got one kiss, it was clear he was going to make it a good one—one that lingered.

The idea of him desiring her, touching her, gave her full-body tingles. When his lips met hers, it was only with the barest of feather-light touches.

One kiss was not going to be enough for her.

Carefully, he touched his lips to hers. The hand on her shoulder slid up to her neck and his thumb traced her jaw. Jasper moved in, his body coming closer to hers.

For a moment, Callie froze.

They'd been together in the most intimate of ways a man and woman could. But she'd never kissed him. But she kissed him now, returning the force of his lips with her own. He parted her lips and kissed her as if to claim her, and brought her against his body with a tight grip. She brought her arms around his sides, and felt the rough fabric of his jacket on her fingers.

Hot damn, but Jasper could kiss.

She was mad at herself for not doing this months earlier. Parts of her stirred that she'd imagined locked away for good.

Kissing meant something as far as Callie was concerned. There'd been very few men in her life that she'd actually allowed to kiss her. Hank, for one. She'd been so taken with him she'd followed him from Fort Worth to the dusty little town of Cricket Bend in the first place. But Hank had proven to be like so many other men, and another woman had caught his attention, and he'd moved on from Callie and left her alone. Jack Braxton had picked up the pieces of her sadness when Hank had stopped looking at her the way he always had. Braxton had even promised to marry her, but then he'd up and vanished one day and that was that.

Men were not reliable creatures. It wasn't in their nature. They were like dogs, always off sniffing at something. But Jasper, he was something else.

True to his word, he pulled back at the conclusion of the kiss.

"That's enough now," he said. "I best stop while I still can."

"Oh jeepers," she said. "What time is it?"

"Nearly eleven, I reckon." His hand was still on her face, his fingers resting on the side of her neck. She could have melted into him right there and not cared.

Matthew cleared his throat loudly, and waited a moment before he and Haven stepped out of the house. Callie blushed a bit at the idea that everyone inside knew full well what they were doing, and were warning them of their impending approach.

"We're going to head home," Matthew said.

Haven couldn't hold back a sneaky smile.

"I should take Nate home," Callie said, going to step into the house.

"He's sound asleep," Haven said with a smile. "Doc sang him a few songs and he passed right out on the rug."

"All that fishing," Matthew said.

Haven stepped toward Callie and touched her arm. "We'll hang up posters tomorrow."

"Sounds fine," Callie said. "Good night."

The Franks headed out. Callie and Jasper went inside the house. Nate had curled up in a wooden rocking chair and was asleep, and Doc was dozing as well. He woke and rubbed his eyes as Callie and Jasper came inside.

"Little bug is sleeping hard," Jasper said.

"Fell right asleep during 'Lorena,'" Doc said. "I think I best get on back before I do the same."

Callie stepped toward Nate to wake him, but Jasper took hold of her elbow.

"Whyn't you let him sleep? I'll bring him in with me in the morning."

"Are you sure?"

Jasper looked at the little boy. "I don't mind a bit. And he loves riding Dorothy. I'll be in early." He scooped Nate up and carried him into the smaller of the bedrooms, then laid him down on the bed. As Callie turned to leave the room, she saw the way Jasper pulled the blankets up over the little boy. It was a kind gesture, and a downright fatherly one.

Callie's heart felt like it was being squeezed. Nate had a father already, though she hadn't realized it.

As she and Doc rode back to town, they didn't speak much.

"Jasper asked me to dinner tomorrow," she said out of nowhere.

"Good for him," Doc answered. "Bring Nate by my place. I'll watch him for you. He likes my singing. I'm proud of Jasper. It takes nerve to ask out a woman, especially one you care about."

"I don't know what I'm doing," she confessed. "And I'm not used to not knowing. I'm used to being bossy and loud and telling folks what to do."

"Maybe you don't have to be the boss of him," Doc said. "Jasper's a fine, capable man."

What an interesting idea. She and Jasper had been dancing around the idea of being together for a long time, both determined to take the lead. What would it hurt if she simply…let him? She touched her lips and remembered the sweet little kiss they'd shared. There'd been nothing wrong in it.

Nothing held Callie back from even more of the happiness Jasper could bring.

Except herself.

"I didn't plan to wind up a bachelor," Doc said. "There was a time I thought I'd get married and be the happiest man ever to walk the earth."

Callie knew little to nothing about Doc's past, so she listened close.

"When I was working on the soldiers, during the war, there was a woman—a nurse. She was the prettiest little thing I'd ever seen, and smart as a whip. Better at doctoring than I was, by far. I worked by her side every day, and I fell for her so hard I could hardly see straight."

Knowing he hadn't wound up with the woman, Callie asked a question she didn't necessarily want to hear the answer to. "What happened to her?"

"War happened," he said. "So many died in that damned war, and she was one of them."

"I'm sorry."

"I didn't tell you that for your pity, Callie girl. I told you because there's a chance standing in front of you for real happiness, and a damn good life, and if you don't take it…well, if you don't take it you're no better than those hens at the Women's Society.

They cluck and get their feathers ruffled over every little thing because they're not happy, most of them."

"I want to be happy."

"Then be happy. Go to dinner with Jasper. Let him court you. He'll do right by you, and he loves Nate with all the love a father could give a child."

"I see that now."

"I know you do."

Callie smiled. "Hell, Doc, you're like my fairy godmother."

"I can't do magic, but I can tell you the honest truth. Don't let him go, Callie girl. No, sir. Don't you dare let him go."

His words stayed with her as she reached the saloon, and went upstairs in a daze.

She had a date with Jasper. A real date.

Heavens to Betsy.

He'd been a different man when she'd met him; foolish, prone to spending all his money on drinking and women. He'd certainly spent enough money on her. Callie closed her eyes at the memories. She and Jasper had certainly had good times back in those days, but that wasn't how she wanted him to think of her, to remember her. He'd been one of those men she hadn't minded visits from as much as the others. Jasper was always clean and kind, even sweet.

Callie went to her wardrobe. Once, it had been full of the clothes she'd worn in her previous profession, but now her dresses were respectable, a striking contrast in colors and cuts.

How long had it been since she'd felt pretty?

When she'd taken over the saloon, she'd packed up her fancy dresses and purchased a whole new set:— darker-colored, higher-cut, and more respectable, the kind Haven wore. Callie still found the dresses stuffy and stifling, but she wanted to look the part, and by looking the part she'd gained some slow respect from some of the other business owners of Cricket Bend. Delia Lance, the widow who ran the restaurant, and Tom Harmon from the hardware store were her closest neighbors, and they'd come to call in recent months, to try and work together to solve the problem of patrons of all three establishments tying their horses back behind the buildings and then not cleaning up after the animals. To do so, they'd set a schedule of hourly checks out the back of the buildings. Knowing the business owners were watching seemed to keep patrons in line.

Horse dung.

Callie had spent so much time thinking about horse dung.

She needed a night to feel like a woman.

Though she'd packed up her old things, she hadn't gotten rid of them. They were all packed into a trunk beneath her bed, and she dropped to her knees and pulled it out. The fluff and feathers nearly burst when she unlatched the hook, and the colors of her old life swarmed around her, the smell of the flowery perfume she'd always worn, and the delicate lace and satin garments she'd worn. Looking at them now, she saw how revealing they'd been. No wonder she'd been so successful.

Jasper had liked her then, but he still liked her

now.

She couldn't very well go out with him wearing one of her old dresses.

But no one would notice what she wore underneath.

And if Jasper happened to find out, would he not be appreciative?

In her wardrobe, she had a fantastic green dress. Cut high and fitted well, she'd bought it for the sole purpose of walking into a meeting of the Women's Society two years prior when Ellie Graham and her harpies had been ready to outlaw Callie from the town. She'd gone in, had a fine time starting trouble, and made an exit before Ellie could burn her at the stake. Haven had come out of the meeting with her, the first time the two women had really recognized the other as a friend.

Callie hadn't worn the dress since. It was beautiful.

She would wear that.

She dug deep in her trunk until she found a pair of stockings and a garter. She'd forego petticoats and bloomers for the night. Her figure was still impressive even after having a baby, and she looked at herself in the mirror. She pulled the pins from her hair and let the waves of yellow fall over her shoulders.

Somewhere under all the responsibility, there was still a woman.

And the woman was going to have a night out tomorrow.

CHAPTER NINE

Jasper

Before the sun was barely over the horizon, Luke and his deputies were riding to the Fowler and Gorman land boundary. The two men refused to meet at each other's homes. They wouldn't even step on the others land, despite a friendship of some thirty years and a bi-weekly game of cards that had been going on longer than Jasper had been alive.

Nope, they sent word to Luke that they wanted to meet on the piece of land causing all the fuss. Horace Gorman and Sam Fowler had been friends for decades, and the rift between them was starting to trickle into town. Mrs. Fowler slipped from the general store when the Gorman boys came in, and the Gormans glared at the Fowlers when they passed in the street.

Jasper gave Dorothy a quick stroke on the neck and sent a prayer to the sky that the situation could be resolved peacefully and quickly.

After all, he had a date with Callie that night.

And nothing, come hell or warring farmers, was going to keep him from it.

Sure as shooting, the men were already there—divided in two groups, neither stepped on the opposite side's land.

In the middle of the contested plot, there stood a table and two chairs.

"We havin' a picnic?" Jasper asked.

"My idea," Luke said. "I thought I could get them to sit and talk it over like reasonable men."

"Has it worked?"

"Nope."

As the lawmen rode up, the groups came together but kept distance between them. Matthew took the leads of the three horses and tied them to part of the Fowler fence.

"They ain't said a word," he muttered. "Not the whole time. None of them."

The lawmen stepped up to the table.

Luke looked at the Gormans for a long moment, then at the Fowlers. No one else moved, or seemed to breathe.

"Mornin', boys," Luke said.

Those two simple words seemed to strike a match.

"You tell Gorman to stay the hell off my property."

"It ain't your property, you old fool."

"Don't call my pa a fool."

"Mind your damned business!"

Words tumbled over words. The distance between the two groups of men shortened as a few steps here and there started to bring them together.

Of the men Jasper recognized, he saw Jeb Gorman was the chief instigator on his side. A ruddy-faced man with a brown beard, Jeb was barrel-chested and wore suspenders and a shirt with rolled-up sleeves. He was a wall of hard-earned muscle topped with a foul scowl, and not someone a man would want to pick a fight with.

He was face-to-face with Seth Fowler, the same age and just as tanned from outside work. Seth had a few inches advantage on Jeb, but they looked evenly matched.

"Your daddy always let you fight his battles?"

"He'd knock you to the ground in two seconds."

"You wanna try?"

"Calm down now," Luke hollered. "This is a land dispute over fifty feet of bad soil. No sense throwing punches and drawing blood."

"It's Gorman land," Jeb called.

"It's Fowler land," Seth shot back.

"Shut your mouths, all of you." Luke held out his hand. "I want all the deeds and maps all of you got on this table right now."

Papers were brought to them. Luke spread the maps out across the table in front of him, and handed Matthew the other papers. Jasper took a wad from Matthew and started reading. Most of it was just letters and other correspondence, pieces of paper that meant nothing.

Seth spit in Jeb's direction. One of Jeb's brothers held him back.

"They gonna behave?" Jasper asked.

"Doubt it," Luke said. "Keep an eye open."

Matthew held up a paper. "Gorman's deed is

from '68."

"Fowler's is from '67. That puts him here first."

"But he can't farm this land. He has to know that. He's just being a stubborn coot."

"That ain't our place."

Jeb Gorman paced back and forth, his eyes never leaving the Fowlers. The man was spitting mad, a bull about to charge. Jasper couldn't help but notice the way Sam Fowler looked at the younger man, with pure murder in his eyes. He never glared at Horace Gorman the same way. The two older men headed up their respective sides, but the fight didn't seem to be about them.

"I think this is about more than fifty feet," Jasper said.

"I think so too," Luke said. "But I don't know what it is."

Jasper thought fast. "Laura Harper's maiden name was Gorman, wasn't it?"

"She was Laura Gorman before she married." Luke looked up at him. "What're you thinking?"

Jasper sighed. "Thinkin' I might talk to Ellie. See if she knows anything about it."

"You want to talk to Ellie?"

"Nope, but I will."

"Think they could keep from killing each other for another day or two?" Matthew nodded to the group. "Jeb looks ready to brawl."

"They'll have to," Luke said. He held up the deeds. "I'm going to check these with the bank too, before I make any decisions. And I'll talk to Doc and Hill and the boys, see what they remember about '67 and '68 out here." He stood up and turned to the group.

Just at that moment, all the logic in the world didn't amount to a hill of beans. Seth Fowler couldn't restrain himself anymore and lunged from behind his father and took a swing at Jeb Gorman, and it was like dynamite went off. Men were on men, punching and brawling, and the three lawmen stood stupid for a moment and just watched the battle erupt.

Luke shouted, "Hey!"

No one heard him over the clamor. Matthew flew into the fight, pulling pairs of men apart and throwing them to the ground. Going in was foolish, but Matthew seemed to relish the chance to throw some men around, and no one was dumb enough to try and hurt a deputy. Jasper moved to follow him, but Luke grabbed his coat. "Don't. Give me one of those chairs."

Jasper did, and Luke stepped up on it, then up on the table, and hollered, "Hey!"

The brawl continued.

"Goddammit." Luke sighed. Calm and cool, he pulled his pistol from his belt and fired one shot into the air.

That stopped things.

"Next man who throws a punch will be spending the next week in my jail," Luke called. "This is a matter of fifty feet of rocky dirt. No sense anyone gettin' hurt."

Not many men in the world scowled as ugly as Jeb Gorman. The man took two steps forward.

"Go home, Anderson. This has nothing to do with that patch of dirt. No need for you boys to be involved."

"I won't allow this kind of behavior in my territory."

Jeb's attitude irked Jasper, so he stepped between Jeb and the table where Luke stood.

Jeb glared up at the sheriff. "I'd like to see you stop it."

Defiant and furious, Jeb wound up and punched Jasper right in the face. Pain shot through Jasper's head and he stumbled backward. Of all the dumb moves, he hadn't expected that. It seemed Matthew had. He came from the crowd and landed on Jeb in a moment, his arm around the rancher's neck. His boys stepped to come to his rescue, but Luke aimed his gun.

"Jeb's gonna come with us and sit in jail for a spell. Anyone who feels like joining him is welcome to do so."

The men fell silent. Jasper recognized how smart Luke was to play it this way—if the Gormans made a move to fight the lawmen, the Fowlers would be on them in a second.

"Horace and Sam, come here," Luke said. It was a demand, not a request. Luke was done with these games. "The rest of you, get back to work. You got farms to run, don't you?"

Horace Gorman and Sam Fowler came to opposite sides of the table, glaring at each other. The two patriarchs couldn't have been more different: Gorman barrel-chested like his son, and Fowler long and lean.

"Your boys are bein' foolish, and you know it." Luke came down from the table. "What's this about?"

The men deliberately didn't answer.

"That soil is awful. This ain't a fight over that."

Sam Fowler pointed his eyes right at Horace Gorman. "If Jeb Gorman would stay away from my Carolee, there'd be no problem at all, Luke."

There it was. The truth of the matter. Jasper and Matthew exchanged a look.

Jeb groaned from the ground. "I told you I love her."

"They been sneaking off together at night for a while. She's a sweet girl, and too innocent to be taking up with the likes of him."

"You don't know a thing about me."

"I know you got a reputation I don't want my daughter involved with." Sam Fowler growled. "You don't talk to her again, you hear me?" He looked to Luke. "Hanging around the place, leaving her flowers."

"Carolee wants to be with me too."

"She ain't but barely seventeen."

Jeb stood firm. "I'm going to marry her."

"The hell you will. I'll kill you first."

"You don't threaten my boy."

Luke ignored Jeb and looked between the two fathers. "For the good of all involved, I'm going to need the two of you to come to some arrangements and be at the jail first thing tomorrow morning."

"Or?"

"Or our relationship is about to be a lot less friendly. And you." He looked down at Jeb and wagged a finger. "Mind yourself around Miss Carolee. This situation, the whole of it, is ready to explode, and I don't want no Hatfield and McCoy bullshit in my territory. I'll throw the whole lot of you in a cell and leave you to rot all together. Am I understood?"

It took a moment, but Horace and Sam nodded.

"I want to hear you say it," Luke said. "Don't want there to be any misunderstanding."

"Yes, Sheriff."

"Yes, Sheriff."

"Good." Luke reached down and hauled Jeb up by the arm. "Now, you're coming with us to the jail, and each time you act out of line or say something you ain't supposed to say, I'm going to add a week to how long you'll be there."

"Yes, Sheriff," Jeb said. He didn't need to be prompted.

"How's your eye?" Luke asked.

Jasper shrugged. "My pride hurts worse. Was supposed to have dinner with Callie tonight, but she'll go running if she sees me like this."

"Hell." Matthew smiled. "If she hasn't run away from your ugly mug by now, a bruise ain't going to be the kicker." He hauled Jeb to his feet.

CHAPTER TEN

Hank

The piece of wood stuck half-in and half-out of in Hank's right ring finger made the digit hurt something fierce. He hadn't done it on purpose, getting the splinter. Truly, he hadn't. Though it had happened just after he'd learned that Luke, Matthew, and Jasper had headed out of town.

As he'd been sucking on the wound, he'd happened to see Doc Gray depart his clinic.

Hank Porter was a big believer in happy accidents.

Inside the clinic, Haven stood on a stool to reach some vials on a high shelf in a cupboard. He looked at her for a moment, before she saw him. She was thinner, older, less alive somehow than she'd been before. When he'd known her last, when he'd slipped into the clinic one hot spring day to steal kisses in the storage closet, she'd worn high-button dresses and always twisted her hair up prettily. On this day she wore a plain blue work dress with rolled-up sleeves and her long dark curls were

90

pulled back in a loose tail.

None of it mattered. She could be bald and in rags, and she'd still be Haven.

He knocked on the open door.

She turned and saw him, and raised an eyebrow. "Men have been shot for less than what you're doing right now."

"Nurse Frank, I am injured. I require immediate medical attention." The innocence dripped from his voice. He held up the hand. "I think it might be fatal."

Haven tilted her head. "Did you get a splinter on purpose just to talk to me?"

"What kind of fool would do something like that?"

"The kind of fool who could come back to Cricket Bend even when half the town wants to beat the tar out of him."

"Men do foolish things for all kinds of reasons."

Haven looked at him for a long time. Hank fidgeted under her gaze. How much had she changed? His memories of their time together were vivid, the stuff he'd made into legends in his mind, but what would Haven say if asked to explain what had happened?

"Sit down." She sighed, reaching for a pair of dangerous, big tweezers and a bottle of alcohol. "Put your hand on the table. Palm up." She bent down to take a close look. "That's a big one."

"I remember when you stitched up my arm," he said quietly. "Pulled that piece of glass out like it was nothing."

"And you hollered like a little girl." Haven

smirked. "This won't be quite as bad, unfortunately."

She laid her hand on his forearm to keep him steady, and Hank sucked in a breath at the feel of her skin on his.

He put his other hand on hers.

"I heard about what happened," he said softly. "I was sorry to hear about it."

"People have big mouths," she snapped. "It's no one's business."

"Haven."

"Stop it," she whispered. "Don't you dare come back here and do this. Don't you dare try and make me regret things I don't actually regret. Now, hold still."

She pulled the splinter from his finger with a hard jerk. It hurt like a whip.

"Sweet Father Christmas," he muttered.

Haven stood up. "Keep it clean. You'll live."

"Still the prettiest nurse in the territory, though your bedside manner has all but deteriorated."

"I'm a real nurse now," she said, nodding to the wall of the clinic where a framed certificate hung by the window. "I went to Philadelphia to study just after Matthew and I married."

"I've never been to Philadelphia," he said.

"I thought you'd been everywhere."

"A good many places, but I never venture too far north. Winter doesn't appeal to me."

"We went in summer, and arrived home just in time for fall. It was grand," she said. Her voice trailed off. "Matthew and I explored the city, and ate at fine restaurants, and saw the ocean, and I studied until my eyes hurt. It was a wonderful time."

Seeing her wistful reminded him of old times. Feeling bold, he reached again for her hand and linked his fingers with hers. Haven glanced at their connected hands, but didn't pull away.

"You are just determined to get yourself shot, aren't you?"

"It would be worth it. I still love you."

Haven's eyes got wide. "Don't, Hank."

He started to stand up. He intended to take her into his arms. "You need to know that I—"

"I want you to go." Haven stepped back from him, looking terrified.

She'd kicked him out once before, with a shotgun, after he'd asked her to run away with him. He'd deserved it, and would have deserved the bullet if she'd shot him. The entire reason he'd ever come to Cricket Bend in the first place had been a ruse. He'd made a deal with a devil. He'd get the deed to the saloon and start the life he'd wanted forever, and all he had to do was to seduce the sheriff's pretty daughter and get caught.

But the sheriff had turned out to be Luke Anderson, and his daughter had turned out to be Haven, and the whole thing had gone to hell. Haven, confused and scared about her engagement to Matthew Frank, had nearly given herself to Hank. When he closed his eyes at night, he still remembered the sight of her in the revealing red dress in his room above the saloon, and the feel of her against him for those few moments. He'd kissed her, and meant it as more than just a physical attraction—but she'd woken up as if from a spell and run out of the room and away from him before anything of real consequence could happen.

It was the closest he'd ever been to heaven.

Now she was kicking him out again. He'd done this all wrong, come too fast and without warning and approached too quickly. Of course she was wary of him; he'd be wary of him too. Backing off was best, at least for a while. "You should know that I plan to stay in town a while."

"And what are you planning to do?"

"See that those I care about are taken care of." He meant the words to hit with resonance. Something in Haven had changed, and Callie had given him a hint what it was. "I'm sure you're aware that I include you in that. I brought you something."

"If it's a red dress, you can keep it."

Hank reached into his pocket and pulled out a small object.

"You can't bribe me."

"Take it," he urged.

Haven held out her hand, and Hank set the jewelry into her open palm. No bigger than a penny, the pin was a single blue flower. "I couldn't find a bluebonnet, so I hope a violet will suffice."

The mention of a bluebonnet wiped the frown off her face. Her brow grew lighter, and she bit her lower lip. She remembered, same as he did. She snapped out of her reverie, and closed her fingers around the pin. "Don't waste your time worrying about me. Worry about Callie, and your son."

"I intend to see that they're cared for, I assure

you."

"What's your angle?"

"I have no angle."

Haven scoffed. Blue fabric swirled around her feet as she turned her back to him. "Keep the place where the splinter was clean, and you shouldn't have any problems."

"Thank you for your exceptional care and kindness," he said. He laced the words with sarcasm, angry that his plan hadn't worked as well as he'd hoped.

He left the clinic before he realized she had kept the pin.

CHAPTER ELEVEN

Callie

Jasper wore a gray vest over his green-striped shirt, and had slicked his hair back for the evening. He'd shaved, and his boots were shined. Knowing he cared as much about this night as she did was a nice feeling, to know she mattered to someone.

He also had an unmistakable purple bruise circling his eye.

"What happened?"

"Farmers decided to brawl. Lucky me was standing in the wrong spot."

Callie breezed up to him and touched his eye, but pulled her hand back when he winced. "Do you want a cool cloth to put on it?"

"What I want is to take my favorite girl to dinner," he said.

"That won't heal your eye."

"My eye'll be fine long as it gets to look at you." He offered his arm. "Shall we?"

"We shall," she said.

Cricket Bend only had one real restaurant, and it

sat right next door to the saloon. It was run by Delia Lance, a bustling woman who had become a widow the previous fall but kept at her life and work, determined to keep living. As they entered, Delia waved at them and motioned for them to sit wherever they liked. Jasper led Callie to what he felt was the best table in the room, right by the front windows.

"Evenin', Jasper. Hello, Callie."

"Delia," Callie greeted.

"Special tonight is a beef roast with carrots and potatoes. Beef is from the Fowler ranch. Thought I'd tell you ahead of time because a few customers—Horace's friends—complained."

"I don't much care either way," Callie said. "I'll have the special."

"So will I."

Appearing relieved, Delia headed off to the kitchen.

Callie crossed her ankles under the table. "The Fowlers are a nasty bunch, aren't they?"

"Naw," he said. "They take things real serious when it comes to their ranch. And I don't say I blame them. They've had issues with cattle thieves and coyotes for years. My pa worked for them when he was about my age."

"How is your ma?"

"Good," he said. "Grace is gonna have another baby by Christmas. I'd like to get up there real soon to visit before winter comes."

"Kansas winters aren't friendly."

"No kidding. Mama is doing well. She writes me twice a week no matter what."

"That's good," Callie said. "That must be nice."

"You ever hear from your family?" Surprised, she looked up at him. "You don't ever talk about them."

"I'm not even sure where I'd write to them if I wanted to." She shrugged. "Nate is my family. He's all I need."

Jasper groaned.

"I apologize for my sentiment," Callie said.

"It ain't that," he said. "Look who just came in the door."

Ellie and Charles Graham had come for dinner. Delia showed them to a table on the other side of the room, and Charles held Ellie's chair out for her. She settled, and he took his own seat. Both of them were dressed fine, Charles in a suit like always and Ellie in an expensive-looking pink dress with a small hat. Charles picked up his menu, but Ellie cast a look toward Jasper. When she saw them both looking back, she leaned forward and touched Charles's arm, said something, and when he chuckled she laughed, though the sound was fake.

"Puts on a show, don't she?"

"This will be awkward," Jasper apologized. He shifted in his seat and adjusted his napkin.

"No it won't," Callie insisted. "Look at me, Jasper." He did. "They ain't even there. It's just us. We're the only ones in the whole room."

A sweet smile played on his mouth. "If I'd known she was coming here—"

"Are you two still involved?" Callie looked down at her fingers, but bobbed her head toward Ellie.

"You know about that?"

"Everyone knows, pumpkin. I imagine folks over in Greeley have caught word by now."

"Nope," Jasper replied quickly. "We ain't been that way for a while."

"That's good," she said.

"Is it?"

"Being involved with a married person is just asking for trouble. Is that why you ended it?"

"How do you know it was me who ended it?"

Callie smiled. "Ellie keeps sneaking looks your way. I know that look."

"What look?"

"The look you send my way every chance you get."

"I keep hopin' someday you'll look back."

Delia arrived with two plates of steaming hot food. The woman had a good cook, and the dinner was delicious. They kept the conversation to the topics of their lives, the issue with the farmers, Nate, the saloon, and treaded gently around the subject of Hank, Haven, and Matthew. Callie didn't care to speak of things that could be unpleasant. There'd be enough time for that in the daylight, but this night was to be enjoyed and savored.

The oil lamp on the table lit up Jasper's face. She studied him as he cut a piece of beef. He wasn't good-looking the way Hank was; noticeable from across a room with a heart-stopping kind of handsome. Jasper's good looks came from a combination of gentle features and the biggest heart in all of Texas, and every piece of him she got to know made him look better and better to her.

"You feel like takin' a walk?" he asked. "Or do you have to get back?"

"Doc said he'd keep Nate as long as I needed," she said. Then she blushed at the implication of Doc's suggestion, knowing Jasper would understand the same. Doc, like everyone else in the whole town, wanted this relationship to happen. "I would very much like to take a walk with you."

"Figure we could walk down by the creek," he said. "It's real pretty at night."

"You know, I've lived here going on three years and I've not been out that way," she confessed. "I stick mostly to town."

"You been missin' out," he said.

"I think I have." On a whole lot of things, she realized.

Jasper paid Mrs. Lance for dinner, which they both complimented highly.

"You mind if we stop by the Graham's table for a moment?" Jasper said. "I got an idea Ellie or her ma might know something about the farmers. Maybe she can shed some light on things."

"I don't mind if you don't mind."

"If we go together, we're safer," he whispered. "I think the two of us could take her in a fight, if need be."

"I'm not so sure about that," Callie joked back. "I bet she fights mean."

Jasper took her hand as they crossed the restaurant to where the Grahams sat, eating mostly in what appeared to be total silence. Ellie perked right up at their approach.

"Miss Lee," Charles greeted, rising from his seat.

"Mr. Graham."

Charles smiled broadly. "I've been meaning to stop by your place. I hear we're competitors."

"I wouldn't say that," she said. "Just didn't want you to have too easy of a time with no contest."

He laughed. "Thank you for keeping me on my toes."

"You're welcome."

"Deputy, I understand there was some trouble today."

"Men being stubborn," Jasper replied. "They're like to get themselves killed." He looked at Ellie. "Sheriff thinks there's something else going on, and I wondered if you or your ma might know anything."

"Anything about a piece of dirt?"

"Anything about why Horace Gorman and Sam Fowler are letting a piece of dirt ruin thirty years of friendship."

Ellie acted coldly. "I wouldn't know."

"I will speak to Laura." Charles spoke to Jasper, but Callie saw him throw a disapproving look down to Ellie, who sat with folded hands. "My mother-in-law seems to know everything about everything most of the time. I'm not sure if it will do any good, but maybe she can put a stop to the fighting at least."

"If you think it could help, we'd appreciate it," Jasper said.

"That from them?" Charles pointed at Jasper's eye.

"Yep."

Charles nodded. "I will relay the message to

Laura in the morning." He winked at Callie. "She is a tenacious woman, to say the least."

"Thank you," Jasper said. "You two have a good evening."

"You as well," Charles said.

Callie bid them farewell. Ellie never even looked at her.

Jasper led her from the restaurant, and around the back and away from town in the shortest path to the creek. "That wasn't near as unpleasant as I'd thought it would be."

"Charles wouldn't be a bad mayor," Callie said.

"Then why'd you choose to run?"

"He's a rich man," she said. "I don't want Cricket Bend to become a place where it's better to be rich than to be anything else. Most of us around here aren't made of money. Most are just trying to get by and raise our families and live a good life."

"That's as good a reason as any."

"I hope people can look past what I used to be," she whispered. He watched her look in the direction of the restaurant. "Some of them never will."

"Don't you worry about Ellie," Jasper said.

"She practically runs the Women's Society. If you think men's wives don't have a big influence on who they vote for, you're crazy in the head."

They were a ways from town, but he hadn't let go of her hand and she hadn't tried to pull free. It felt nice to be affectionate, to feel another's skin on hers. Funny how the simple act of holding a hand could feel as intimate and important as more private acts.

Walking in the dark with Jasper was dangerous.

Any lines she'd been determined not to cross had already blurred, and being alone with him, with his hand touching hers, was setting her head to spin. Callie liked men, and liked the feeling of being with one who knew what a woman needed. Beside her, Jasper looked straight ahead. His expression was calm, relaxed. Damn the man. If he was thinking what she was thinking, he sure wasn't letting it rattle him the way she was.

Up ahead, a big willow tree hung over part of the creek, and they walked in that direction.

The silence between them allowed her a chance to listen to the sounds of the earth. They walked along the edge of the creek. Callie listened to the soft splashes of waves hitting rocks and water making its way down the creekbed. She heard the sound of the grass brushing and bending beneath their feet. Mostly, though, Callie heard the hum of the crickets.

"They're so loud out here."

"You don't hear them as much in town anymore, on account of all the people and noise. But they haven't gone anywhere. They get so loud out by my place, that once in a while they wake me up."

She smiled. "Such a tiny little bug."

"That's what I call Nate. Bug."

"I know. It fits. He's tiny, but he makes a racket when he wants to. Like a cricket."

"Can I ask you something?"

Callie shrugged. "I suppose so."

"Why'd you turn to it?"

"What?"

"The…working upstairs."

"Are you sure you want to hear about that?"

He didn't answer, and she didn't blame him.

"I didn't turn to it. It wasn't really a choice. I just didn't know how to do anything else." Jasper looked at the dirt. Callie continued walking. It was easier to talk when she was moving. "My folks were poor as could be, and they had a lot of us. Didn't see much point in sticking around to work my fingers to the bone and starve along the way, so I up and left when I was too young to be leaving, thinkin' I knew better than anyone else. But I made my way. Worked at a mill for a little bit, but it was exhausting and I couldn't breathe. Men told me I was pretty and wanted to take me to dinner and buy me things, so I started to let them and it was nicer than working…next thing I know I'm in Fort Worth with Hank Porter, Emma is up onstage singing her heart out, there's a poker table covered in money, and little me is the life of the party."

Those had been the days. She remembered the silk and flowers, the jewels and card games. Some of the faces of the men she'd known along the way came back to her, bringing memories both good and bad. All the memories led her to one conclusion. "And then one day, Hank suddenly had the deed to a saloon in some little town a ways east, and we packed up and, ta-da, I'm standing in Cricket Bend."

"We'd never seen anything like you before," he said. "At least, I hadn't."

She laughed out loud. "Oh, I believe that."

They took a few more steps, side-by-side.

"You ever get hurt?"

She would not deny it. It had been a part of her life. Things got rough sometimes between clients and girls. "Everyone gets hurt."

"I'd never hurt you."

"That is the one thing in this world I know to be true," she said.

They'd reached the willow, and Jasper pushed some strands aside so they could duck underneath.

"My my, Mr. Tanner, what a scandalously secret place you've led us to."

Jasper took her other hand in his. Holding both of them, he stepped close to her and she had to look up to see his crystal-clear brown eyes. "That ain't why I brought you here. I'm happy just to talk to you."

"I like talking to you," she said. "I know my past isn't—"

"Hush," he said. "It don't matter."

"It does," she insisted. "I know it bothers you sometimes. It'd bother any man."

"You're always talking about all men as if we're the same."

"For most of my life, I didn't see any difference. The men I've known all only wanted one thing from me in the end, no matter what they promised."

"You talking about Braxton?"

Callie squeezed her eyes shut and threw back her head. "Dammit, Jasper."

The name had broken the spell of the moment. Regret and shame flooded back to her.

"I don't like him," Jasper blurted. "I'll admit it. A man sweeps in, makes promises that get you all dreamy and happy, and then runs off and doesn't come back, and you're still holding out hope for him? It's a fool's notion, Callie."

"I am not holding out hope for him anymore."

"Sure you're not."

"I'm not," she insisted.

"What changed?"

So much had changed, but one thing most of all. "You did."

As if all he'd needed from her was a reassurance that her feelings were the same as his, Jasper bent forward and reached to surround her. Callie fought the urges of her body to jump on him and go with the night, but put a hand on his chest.

"Let me kiss you," he muttered. "It's all I've been thinking about since the other night. That one kiss wasn't enough."

"Maybe it has to be," she answered firmly.

"You don't mean that."

"Dammit." Frustration at her multitude of feelings made her frown.

"You gonna be mad at me for wanting you? Lord. I think the world of you, Callie. I'm happy to do nothing but talk until the sun comes up, but it won't stop me from wanting you. Men have needs, you know." Jasper shrugged.

"Women have them too."

His eyes flared for a moment and he took a deep breath. "If you were trying to turn me off, that didn't help."

"I'm not—" Callie let a sound of frustration and put a hand to her hair. "Jeepers."

"Callie…"

"What?"

She whirled to face him, and Jasper had moved closer. He stood, arms folded over his chest, waiting. "Kiss me." When she didn't answer, he continued. "You care for me just as much as I care for you."

"I do."

"Then let's stop dancing around it."

He'd been there for her, for Nate, for Matthew, for Haven, for everyone. If he'd been a foolish youth, he'd grown into a man worth being proud to be with, a man she'd be proud to be kissing. He'd helped her so many times. He'd even single-handedly stopped Andrew McKenzie from escaping the saloon after he'd tried to murder Emma Porter.

And Callie's whole body, the deceitful beast, yearned for him.

They were away from town. The night was dark and clear, and stars shone overhead. The willow tree would provide fine cover, not that there was anyone around to be covered from.

In two steps, she was pressed close to him. He didn't budge from his position, so she put her hands on his strong arms and rose up to put her lips on his. She kissed him, and he kissed her back.

And then his arms came unfolded, and enfolded her tight against him. Swept up, Callie let her hands roam his chest and shoulders, coming to rest around his sides. Jasper's hands slid down her back to her bottom, and he took handfuls of her skirt to hold her against him.

"Curse you for being so good at kissing," she managed to say.

"You're not so bad yourself," he answered.

She laughed, then gasped as Jasper brought his lips to her ear. The high neck of her dress blocked him from doing much else, and Callie reached up to unhook a few of the top buttons. When the fabric was out of the way, he took to kissing her neck. The sensation of his breath against her skin had her wiggling in pleasure, pressing parts of her body against parts of his that were both incredibly scandalous and incredibly exciting.

Jasper dropped to his knees and slid his hands down the whole length of her until he was kneeling in the grass. He held out a hand for her. "Come to me."

A light breeze touched her cheek, cooling her warmed skin.

He put out his hand and touched the side of her knee through her skirt, looking up at her with the eyes of a man on fire.

The hunger and need inside her that cried out for him could be satisfied easily.

So Callie knelt down too. His hand slid up to her waist, holding on with firm fingers. Face-to-face, he whispered, "We can go slow."

"When have we ever gone slow?"

"I don't want to scare you away."

She threw her arms around his neck and practically tackled him with the hard force of desire, knocking him back into the dirt and covering him in kisses. Jasper didn't fight one bit as she moved herself on top of him, her lips staying with his. He moved his hands to her thighs, and took hold of her skirts.

When her skirt came up over her thighs, Jasper's

eyes grew wide.

"You ain't wearing—"

"Nope. Just stockings."

"Damnation," he breathed. "You planned on this?"

"I hoped for this."

His hands went to his belt, and he quickly undid it as Callie reached for the buttons of his shirt. She wanted to be able to touch him, to feel his skin under her fingertips. Once she'd opened it, she pushed the fabric aside. He was finely formed, muscled from the work of building a house and maintaining it. The crisp hair on his chest traced a line down his body, and she let her fingers follow it until she'd reached his manhood.

He grunted as her fingers surrounded him. "Callie—"

"Hush," she said. "Don't you say a thing unless you want me to stop."

"Nope," he said. "No, ma'am, I do not want that at all."

"I didn't think so."

She spit on her fingers and took hold of him. Pleasing him was all she cared about, and watching the way his face changed under her touch, she knew she was doing just that. Shifting, she joined their bodies, and Jasper cursed a whisper in the dark.

Damn, but she liked men. Despite all the mean things she spouted about them, they still had at least one necessary purpose.

Callie ran her fingernails over Jasper's chest, wishing she could keep the vision forever of the blissful expression on his face. The good feelings she stirred up were shared, and both moaned at her movements. Jasper's fingers clutched her thighs, digging in hard.

She rocked harder, observing which rhythm stirred him the most. He didn't mind if she moved fast, but when she slowed and increased her force he looked ready to go crazy with desire. She made her own pleasure, skilled at doing just that from so many years of practice, and soon hollered out in delight into the emptiness of the night.

Jasper shifted as if he would roll them over, but Callie held him down and leaned forward to kiss him. He stopped trying, and returned to enjoying himself. She wanted that. She wanted him to like it, wanted to see his face melt with pleasure again.

Jeepers. Being with a man she loved was—

Callie gasped at the realization. She loved him.

***

Jasper

The woman was a twister. He'd seen her coming, the way she'd looked at him a few times during dinner as if she wanted what she couldn't have. He'd deliberately aimed for the willow, not in an attempt to get under her skirts but in the hopes that she'd open up to him if they weren't surrounded by the everyday bustle of town.

It had worked better than he'd expected.

Flat on the ground, she moved in ways that stirred up all the desire he'd ever felt for her. Her fingertips grazed his chest, her sweetness joined with his own body, and it took all of Jasper's self-control not to lose his mind right then and there.

She'd taken her pleasure from him, mostly by herself with no need of his help. He'd remedy that, he vowed, but for now his own was growing closer. Callie bent forward to him, and he felt the soft pieces of her hair that had escaped from her twist brushing his face.

Slipping his hands over the silky dress, he brought his hands to her bottom and held hard as she bounced a few more times, then moved her mouth to the side of his face and bit his ear.

He moved fast and took himself from her and sat up to spill his seed on the ground. She remained on top of him, holding his head tight against her chest until his body had quaked and settled again.

"You are incredible," he whispered in her ear. He meant it.

Callie moved herself to one side of him and pulled her skirts down over her legs. She didn't look at him, and he felt a twitch of fear. Something had changed, again. The eyes he'd watched tease and rejoice only moments earlier were now scared.

"Hey." Jasper reached for her, but she stood up.

"We shouldn't have done that," she said, trying to convince herself, he figured.

"Why not?"

"We—"

"We what?"

"We've done it before."

"Not like this we haven't."

"Shut up."

Being scared made her ornery. He got to his feet

111

and hooked his pants. "I know what you mean. Yes, we've done that before. Yes, back when it was something else completely. But if you'd like, we could start anew."

"You mean pretend like none of it ever happened?"

"Nope. I ain't ashamed of what happened in the past. I mean we could get married—now. You know how I feel about Nate. I'd be glad to be the boy's father. And believe me, I'd be even happier to be your husband."

"Jeepers." Callie's response was barely audible.

Jasper waited. "I been thinkin' about asking you for a while now."

"I appreciate everything you've done for me, and for Nate."

"But—"

"But?" He hadn't really figured she would say no, but what if she did?

"I'll need some time."

"Of course." It wasn't the reaction he'd hoped for. He'd imagined it going differently, that she'd leap into his arms and they'd live the rest of their lives happy as one of the fairy tales Nate liked to listen to before bed.

Carefully, he stepped toward her and touched her cheek, then kissed her on the forehead. "I'll wait, Callie. You're worth waiting for. Come on. I'll get you home."

The walk back to town was silent. Jasper took her to Doc's, where they retrieved a sleeping Nate, and bid the two of them good night outside the saloon doors.

A light shone from the jail.

Jasper found Matthew sitting at his desk staring at the tabletop covered in papers.

"Evenin'" he said.

Matthew looked up, surprised out of whatever daydream he'd been lost in. "How'd it go?"

"It went," Jasper said. "It went somewhere."

"A good somewhere or a bad somewhere?"

"I feel like I should say good, but…women are a mystery, Matthew."

"That's the honest truth."

"I talked to Charles and Ellie. Charles said he'd mention the feud to Laura tomorrow, see if she knows anything."

"Ellie didn't know anything?"

"Ellie looked at me and Callie like we was a couple of lepers."

"Of course she did," Matthew said. "The woman's jealous as can be. Watch out for her."

Jasper scoffed. Ellie was a pain in the ass, but harmless. "I best get home. I'll see you in the morning."

He reached the livery—where Dorothy was and where he needed to go to start making his way home—and walked past it before going inside. Out back was a pile of crates, and after looking to make sure no one was around, he kicked one. It felt good, so he kicked another. And another. One broke into pieces when it hit the wall, and he didn't care.

Never had a man been more frustrated after being so sweetly satisfied.

Callie had wanted him, and Lord but she'd had him. Right in the dirt, before God, she'd taken him with such ease he'd figured she'd wanted him. She had to have wanted him, or why would she have done it?

He went into the stable, and hauled Dorothy's saddle onto her.

He was cinching her when arms slipped around him in the darkness.

The arms did not belong to Callie, though for a moment he hoped they did. Jasper knew it in an instant from the smell of the perfume and the way the arms didn't have the softness of Callie's. They weren't the arms he wanted to be holding him, and the woman who'd sneaked into the barn to meet him wasn't the one he wanted her to be.

"I missed you," Ellie Graham cooed into the darkness.

Jasper pulled her arms off him and stepped away. "For God's sake, stop sneaking up on men in barns. You'll get yourself shot one of these days."

"Are you mad at me?"

"I ain't mad at you," he said. He tried to bring his voice down. His frustration that night wasn't her fault. "This just ain't the time."

"There was a time it was always the time."

For all Ellie Graham's fancy clothes and finery, she was a plain woman. Plain was no crime, but her heart was plain. Like her mother, she'd only ever wanted things, prestige, and didn't care about the things that really mattered in life. If she'd thought of them at all, she'd have been home with her husband instead of sneaking into a barn at night chasing Jasper.

They'd been stupid and reckless teenagers

together, the two of them.

He'd even thought he loved Ellie once, a long time ago. In his teenage foolishness he'd sincerely believed he was making love to her each time they sneaked away to a hay loft or the big willow by the bend in the creek.

Tonight, under the willow, he'd known love.

"It's been a long time," she said. He heard the way she changed her voice, kept it low and breathy. Once, the sound of the shift would have made him lose his mind, but no longer.

"Yep."

"I can take your mind off it, whatever is troubling you."

"No, you can't." He chuckled.

"Want me to try? The loft is full of hay. It looks soft as can be up there."

It had been their way, to sneak to a hay loft under cover of night. Those nights had been fun, and even after she'd married Charles they'd continued now and again, two stupid fools only thinking about themselves. Now the idea didn't even appeal to him.

"No," he said in a stronger tone. "Go home, Ellie. Go home to Charles."

"This is because of her, isn't it?"

"Ellie—"

"You've fallen for the whore."

"Her name is Callie and you know it. Go home."

Ellie laughed loud, and the sound crackled. "You've actually fallen for her. Women like that don't fall in love, Jasper. They just use men to get the things they want."

115

"That ain't true."

Ellie's eyes grew wide. "She's got you right where she wants you."

"I don't know what you're talking about. Callie could have any man she wanted."

"Don't you see it, Jasper? She wants you because I want you. She's using you."

"And how are you any different?" He turned on her. "You're not here with me because you care for me. You're here with me because she cares for me and you can't handle that. You're lying and jealous."

"Of Callie Lee."

"So you do know her name."

"I know more than that. I know where you went tonight. That willow was our place."

Jasper groaned in irritation. "Every young couple in town thinks that willow is their place," he answered.

"You ruined it," she said with a crack in her voice. "It's tainted now, because of her. Do you have any idea how many men—"

"I have never hit a woman in my life, Ellie, but if you don't shut up and go home I might change my entire life philosophy."

"You're just changing all over the place." She spit. "There was a time you'd have thrown me down in that hay and not argued one bit."

"Things change. The sooner you realize that, the better for both of us."

Ellie's eyes narrowed, and she hiked up her skirt to stomp from the barn.

When she was gone, Jasper kicked at the dirt.

Two women was too much for a reasonable man to handle.

Ellie being mad at him didn't bother him as much as the way she'd spoken of Callie. It was a problem he had; walking down the street, seeing the other men in town, and wondering how many of them had known Callie in that way. He knew it had happened, that she had had other clients, but the idea of other men having put their hands on her churned his stomach. The images that came to mind hurt, and he squeezed his eyes shut to block them out; Callie with other men, doing the things she'd done with him as if she wasn't worth waiting for a man who would deserve her.

He wanted her, all for himself.

And she'd kissed him. She'd gone to the ground with him and had wanted him too. It was just her damn stubborn belief that men weren't worth a hill of beans standing in their way, a belief she'd hard-earned through a life of dealing with men who weren't reliable.

Callie wasn't using him. That was the trouble. She was fighting a war of thoughts and feelings in her head about what her future could hold. If she'd been using him, she'd be better at it.

No, sir. Callie Lee had genuine, bona fide feelings for him.

In the darkness of the barn, Jasper smiled. Now all he had to do was get her to come around and realize it.

CHAPTER TWELVE

Callie

Sleep proved fruitless. Callie spent most of the night rolling around in her bed alone, thinking about Jasper. In truth, she'd wanted him just as bad as he'd wanted her. Having a man honest enough to straight up tell her his desires was refreshing, and everything they'd done had felt...jeepers, it had been good. The recollection of his kisses and his hands and his...

"Mama."

Nate had gotten out of his bed and stood in her doorway, teddy bear in hand.

"Hi sugar." She sat up in bed. He ran to her and jumped on her bed, snuggling into her neck.

Callie smoothed Nate's hair back off his forehead while he slept a little longer. The sweetness of his face, the way he pursed his lips while he slept, and the incredible heat that came off him when he dreamed—these were just some of the miracles of motherhood, she'd learned. To love something so small so much so quickly, her heart

118

had nearly exploded the first time she'd laid eyes on him.

Like a mother bear, she would protect Nate until her dying breath. And if she died, she'd come back as a ghost and haunt the bastard even further. Hank Porter was not a terrible man. He had kindness in him, and a sense of loyalty—even if it was a confused sense, and scattered. He was selfish and difficult, sure, but he was not a bad person. But he was no kind of man to be a father.

Jasper was.

"Come on, sugar." She got them both out of bed and dressed for the day. Laying around thinking wouldn't do any good.

It was Sunday. Most of the town would be at church, including Jasper. She took the opportunity to get herself and Nate dressed, and get a picnic packed to spend the better part of the day playing by the creek. They saw field mice and an eagle, and overturned rocks to find bugs. Nate insisted on bringing his new train with him, and had a fine time rolling it over rocks and up the bark of trees.

On Monday morning, Callie and Haven went out to hang up a pile of twenty signs. Nate trailed along, proud as a peacock to be carrying a few posters of his own. They hung one right outside the saloon, of course, and then with Mrs. Lance's permission outside the restaurant. Charles Graham already had signs up. They were bigger and brighter than Callie's and they looked professionally made, but she wouldn't let that bother her.

Money wasn't everything. Just because a man had more money than he could ever spend in a lifetime didn't mean he had happiness. Callie didn't know much about Charles and Ellie Graham's relationship, but she'd seen the look on Ellie's face when Jasper had approached her. Ellie still held a candle for him, and Charles would have to be blind not to notice.

"Callie," Haven said.

She'd been caught up in her thoughts again, and nearly walked right past the flat wall outside the clinic.

"You gonna hang a poster here? Doc said we could."

"Right," Callie said. "Yes, a poster."

Watching Callie out the corner of her eye, Haven picked one of the posters from Nate and held it up to the wall. "You're distracted today."

"Yep."

"Does it have anything to do with you and Jasper going to dinner on Saturday?"

"How—"

"Word travels," Haven said. "Well, Doc told me. Was it nice?"

"It was. It was real nice, in fact."

Haven waited to hear more, and when Callie didn't answer, she understood how much more there was to say, and her dark eyes grew wide. "Callie!"

"What?"

"You and Jasper—"

Callie put a hand on Haven's mouth. Her friend's voice was too loud. "Hush, would you? The people in Georgia don't need to know."

Haven dropped her voice. "Oh my stars. You didn't."

"We did."

Haven squealed. "Where?"

"The Big Willow."

"Tell me everything," she said. "Was he…was it worth it?"

"You dirty-minded scamp."

"I recall you once telling me that women had the same interest and urges in these matters as men." Haven slanted the poster a little to the side so it was even. "Nail this, and don't get prudish on me now. I'm living vicariously through you, so make it good."

Callie tried to figure out how to begin, but something caught her eye.

Carolee Fowler stood a bit off from the jail, trying obviously to pretend she wasn't there or interested in what was happening inside. The tiny thing with the nearly-black hair would take a few steps toward the jail, then one or two the other way, then glance around like she was going to rob a bank. "What's Carolee up to?

Haven knew, of course. "Jeb Gorman is in the jail."

"For punching Jasper?"

"That, and cause Papa wanted to make an example of him for the other farmers."

"So why is Carolee all nervous?"

"I'm not sure. Let's find out."

They looked at each other.

"After all, the girl might be in need of some help."

"And we do need to hang a poster outside the jail."

Callie and Haven nailed up the poster and went to the jail, where Haven held up a poster to the wall and Callie told her to move it to the left. After a moment, they pretended to realize Carolee was there.

"Carolee," Haven greeted.

"Morning, Mrs. Frank."

"You need something from Papa? He's not in there, but Matthew is."

Carolee shook her head quickly. "Nope, I just…"

"You all right, Carolee?"

"Is Jeb doing all right?"

"Jeb Gorman?" Callie looked at Haven. If the pretty Fowler daughter was sweet on Jeb Gorman, a whole lot of things made sense.

Carolee nodded. "He punched Deputy Tanner yesterday, so they hauled him in here."

"Your pa know you're here?"

Carolee shook her head. "I told him I was going to town to get some fabric for a new tablecloth. You're Callie Lee."

"The one and only, I suppose."

Carolee tilted her head a bit. "My cousin Ellie don't like you."

"Your cousin Ellie is a spoiled brat."

Carolee grinned. "Don't I know it?"

Callie laughed. "We were across the street and couldn't help but notice you dancing around like a nervous hen."

Carolee looked relieved to not have to keep up a charade. "I need to talk to Jeb. It's real important."

Haven and Callie exchanged a look. The two women went to either side of Carolee, and all but whisked her away from the jail into the street. Nate hung on to Haven's fingers. "Are you and Jeb sweet on each other?" Haven asked it conspiratorially, as if it were an exciting secret.

Carolee smiled. "We sure are. I can't think of any man as fine as Jeb."

Over Carolee's head, Haven looked at Callie with wide eyes. The silliness of young people in love never failed to amuse, not the least because Haven had only recently been the same. She had made her fair share of mistakes, and if Callie could steer Carolee away from doing the same she would.

"Can I give you a piece of advice earned the hard way?"

"All right," Carolee looked nervous.

"You're young, and you're real pretty. Men are going to be falling over you for a long time. Don't rush into something you might not want in the end."

"I love Jeb."

"And that's fine. But your papa and your brothers—that's more important. Men come and go, but family—that's worth fighting for. Trust me when I say men are trouble, no matter how good they look."

"Amen," Haven said. "And the walking embodiment of that is on his way to us right now."

"Ladies!"

Hank strode up to the trio, a cocky smile on his face. As he got closer, he noticed Carolee.

Callie groaned, seeing it before it started. Carolee was about as pretty as a girl could be, and certainly looked older than her age suggested. Callie had been the same way, and knew what Hank was thinking as he took in the sight of Carolee's rosy cheeks, raven hair, and bursting figure.

"Mrs. Frank, Miss Lee, and though I have not had the pleasure of making your acquaintance, miss, may I just say that you're the prettiest little—"

Haven cleared her throat. "Seventeen," she said under her breath.

Hank got it. "The prettiest little campaign posters I have ever beheld. Astonishing work, ladies. Worthy of hanging in a museum. Are you in need of any assistance?"

"No, thank—"

Haven handed him a poster and some nails. "Yes, actually. Hang that up on that wall over there, would you?"

"Haven!"

"If he's going to follow us around—which we know he is—he can at least be useful. These posters ain't going to hang themselves, and Hank has a good ten inches of height on either of us. I bet Nate'd be all too happy to carry the hammer for you too."

In Haven's tone, Callie did not miss the hint of joviality. If she wasn't happier than she'd been in a long time in Hank's presence, she was at least more relaxed, or at least distracted.

Callie stepped around Hank to Carolee. "Go on home, before you're seen. Don't make more trouble for your folks right now. The boys are ready to start fighting already. You don't want to be the reason someone gets hurt."

Carolee's face twisted a bit. The girl wanted to say something, but just started to walk away. Callie took her arm.

"If you need any help, you let me know."

Her mind was still on Carolee as she and Haven and Hank postered their way down one side of the street and back up the other way to the saloon.

"Haven!"

Luke and Matthew were outside the jail.

"Crud," Haven breathed. She handed Hank the last of the nails. "I have to go."

"Bye," Callie whispered.

Haven went across the street and joined her husband and father. Matthew shot a look of murder across the street to Hank, and Luke didn't look pleased either.

"I keep waiting for the sheriff to shoot me," Hank said.

"Luke is just watching out for Haven. You can't be mad at him for that."

Hank shook his head. "On the contrary. Seeing his devotion to her makes me realize that if I'd had a father like him, I might not have wound up the man I am today."

"Shoot, there are worse men than you."

"Are there?"

Callie was surprised to hear a genuine note of concern and sadness in his voice. "Theo and Andrew McKenzie. Philip Frank. The list is long. You ain't any sort of a saint, of course, but you're no kind of devil. I've known terrible men, Hank, and you ain't one of them."

"Really?"

"Truly." Nate pulled at Callie's skirt and wanted to be picked up, so she did. "Oof, sugar, it's about time for you to have some supper and get to bed. Excuse me, Hank."

"Of course," he said.

Callie started behind the bar, Nate still in her arms.

"Can I read him a story?" Hank said without looking up.

"A story?"

"A bedtime story, later tonight."

"Hank—"

"I want to know him, even if it's just a little bit."

She thought about it. "After we have supper, I'm going to give him a bath. You come on back around seven. He likes *Little Red Riding Hood* the best. Make the wolf's voice scary. He giggles."

"I'm sorry I ran out," Hank said. "That I wasn't there for you and for him."

"We haven't been alone," she answered.

"Being alone in Cricket Bend would be impossible, I'm sure."

"I ain't mad at you."

Hank looked relieved. "Seven o'clock, then."

"And if you want to put yourself back in my good graces, you best bring me a gift too."

Hank smiled. He probably thought she meant Nate's toy train, which the boy hadn't let go of since he'd gotten it. That was all well and good, but Callie wasn't stupid enough to miss the tiny flower pin hooked to the neckline of Haven's dress. It was a purple flower. And Haven had never worn it before.

CHAPTER THIRTEEN

Jasper

How fast a week could pass.

Before Jasper could blink, it was the day of the speeches. He had barely seen Callie in days, not since the night that had gone so beautifully and ended so strangely. She'd been holed up with Haven, or Hank, or Doc, or Nate, or any combination of the four, readying her speech, making connections, and still running a business and raising a child. She hadn't come looking for him, either. If she needed some time to think over his proposal, he'd give her that.

The speeches began as the sun started to set and the day's heat began to fade. Folks, men and women, black and white, gathered around outside the restaurant. The steps there were wider than most other places, and Delia had offered it up. The day was warm, and the flapping of women's colored fans made a pretty landscape against the dusty brown street and wooden buildings.

Jasper saw the Women's Society hens clucking

at each other in a cluster, and Ellie standing right in front of them. They looked like a small army, and she was the commander. Lizzie Wedgewood was among them, to his surprise, but she smiled at him as he walked up next to where Matthew stood.

Jasper looked over the whole town. Hank was off a ways, listening at the edge of the crowd. He saw Jasper and gave a little wave of acknowledgement.

Luke stepped up onto the top step and held up his hands.

"All right," he said. "Evenin', everyone. What we're doing here tonight is letting the candidates for mayor say a few words about why you should vote for them. Election is next week Friday, and you'll be voting at tables outside Harper's store."

"Doc says that's a conflict of interest." Matthew spoke to Jasper without taking his eyes from Luke. "That folks will walk up, intending to vote for Callie, and might be swayed by it being at Harper's store."

"I don't imagine there's any place in town that's not the same."

Jasper saw George and Laura Harper turn and wave to the crowd. He rolled his eyes at the uppity duo. He'd never cared much for Ellie's parents, and they'd sure never cared for him. No doubt they were fully in support of Charles. Their combined influence would be hard to overcome.

Haven scampered up, squeezing between him and Matthew.

"She ready?" Matthew asked.

"Nervous, but as ready as she's gonna be. And

she looks beautiful."

"She's always beautiful," Jasper said.

Haven and Matthew both turned to him with interest.

"Well, beautiful never hurt," Matthew said. "Might get her a couple votes along the way."

Luke clapped his hands together. "Now, being as I'm a gentleman, I think we should let the lady go first."

"Lady," Ellie scoffed loud enough for a lot of folks to hear. "Callie Lee is no lady."

"Shut up," Haven said in response, loud enough for some folks around them to hear.

"Haven," Matthew warned.

"I'm not going to let her act like that."

Ellie glared at her, and Haven glared right back. Jasper felt a fire in his belly. Seeing Ellie's mean streak on display in front of the whole town was jarring. Usually, she kept it inside and feigned civility.

"So, Callie Lee, come on up here."

Callie stepped up to the top step and turned to the gathered citizens. Haven had spoken true: she looked resplendent in a dark blue dress with a trim bodice. Her yellow hair was pulled up and back in a neat twist. If he'd not been in love with her, how would she have appeared, Jasper wondered? The answer was encouraging. She looked respectable, beautiful, and despite the nerves Haven had mentioned, Callie didn't look to be at all scared.

She'd faced down murderers. Giving a speech should be no problem.

"Thank you, Sheriff." Callie beamed at Luke,

then turned it toward the gathered crowd. "Hi everyone."

"Hey, Miss Callie!" Rip Peters waved from the back of the crowd.

"Hi Rip." Already looking friendly, she eased into her speech. "Most all of you know me already. I am a business owner in this town, and I am raising my son here. I've been a lot of places in my life, but Cricket Bend is really the first home I've ever known, and I'm running for mayor in order to help this town grow into all it could be. We've got plenty of fine people living here, and with just a few steps we could attract more good people. The first thing I would do as mayor is ask our business owners, all of them, including myself, to contribute a small percentage of their annual profits to a fund that would be used for improvements to the schoolhouse and jail, since those are things most of us use or are glad to have. It wouldn't be a big amount, so to those of you with businesses don't you worry, but it would help out a lot."

"Was that your idea?" Jasper asked Haven.

"Nope. That one was Hank."

Jasper looked over to where the scoundrel stood, arms folded and grinning. By God, the man was proud of Callie. He'd helped her. That didn't jibe with the Hank Porter Jasper had thought he'd known.

"And I think we should spend more time celebrating and getting to know our neighbors," she continued. "If I'm elected, I'll make sure we have a spring dance and a fall harvest fair. Maybe even a pumpkin pie contest. I'm sure we could find more than a few volunteers to judge, especially if Mrs. Lance and Mrs. Frank sign up to make pies."

"I volunteer," Doc called out immediately.

"Me too," Paul Archer chimed in.

A few more people called out answers, friendly words. Callie was appealing to them in a way Charles Graham couldn't—by being one of them.

"If Mrs. Frank wants a bake-off, I'm game," Delia said. She'd been standing behind Callie, as the speeches were happening outside her establishment, but she stepped forward and aimed her words right at Haven.

"Any day, Delia!" Haven called back.

Callie held up her hands. "Well then, a fall harvest fair it'll be. Now, to be serious for a moment, I won't claim I'm any kind of expert on running a town. I've got a lot to learn. But I promise that if you choose me to be your mayor I'll listen to everyone and do my best to take everyone's opinions into account. I ain't going into this thinking I'll be queen and y'all will jump at my command."

"Do we get free drinks if you win?"

Callie smiled toward Charles Graham. "Tell you what. No matter who wins, drinks'll be on the house on the night of the election."

A cheer went through the crowd. It had been a good move, Jasper thought. She came off looking affable and friendly to her competition.

"Mr. Graham," Luke called.

Charles stepped up, shook Callie's hand, and took the step. "First of all, let me say that I am thrilled Miss Lee has put her hat in the ring for this election. She's a kind lady, and smart as a whip. No matter who wins, I put my full support behind the idea of a harvest fair. I'm glad she's running against me. Folks should have a choice in who leads their town."

Callie blushed a bit, and glanced out at the townspeople.

Her eyes found Jasper's. He winked at her.

Charles continued. "Now, why do I think you should vote for me over her? It comes down to one thing: experience. I have run the bank here in Cricket Bend for twenty years, and I was a clerk on the first day it opened up. This country was coming out of a war back then, and towns were destroyed and shutting down while we were just beginning. Some folks thought it a lunatic's notion to start a town in a territory that saw more trouble than anywhere in Texas did, but we did it, by God. Luke remembers those days, I bet."

"You know it."

"All we had was a couple buildings and a hell of a lot of cows, and a creek with a bend. It was my father who came up with the name Cricket Bend, you know."

Jasper's heart sank a bit. Charles Graham knew what he was doing. His experience was greater than Callie's, and by speaking to Luke he'd made himself even more likable.

But damn, she was a good candidate.

Charles concluded his speech, and there was applause equal to that which Callie had earned. Luke reminded everyone that the election was coming up, and then the speeches were over.

"Gonna be a fight," Matthew said. "They both made good cases."

The crowd began to dissipate. Jasper started to move forward, to seek out Callie and tell her she'd done well. Even if she didn't care to see him, he needed her to know he was proud of her.

"Way I see it, you can vote for a good man with plenty of experience, or you can vote for a whore."

Jasper turned to see who had spoken the vile words, but the crowd was too thick. He didn't recognize the voice, which meant it wasn't Ellie's. Other people felt the same way. Was Callie running for a position she could never have?

"Shut your mouth, Esther."

That voice he recognized. Lizzie Wedgewood was face-to-face with Esther Malloy, looking cross.

"I am just speaking the truth."

"You are speaking cruel words, and you're better than that."

Like Matthew and Haven and Ellie, Lizzie had grown up in Cricket Bend and gone to school with them. She'd been quieter and smarter than most of the other girls, focused on different things, and from that she and Haven had been better friends than most, though Lizzie had been a part of Ellie's Women's Society because that was what proper young women did—grew up, got married, and joined the women's society and Ellie's ranks.

"Are you in favor of her winning over Charles?"

"I am in favor of our mayor being someone who really gives a damn about this town."

Apparently Lizzie was breaking rank.

Jasper joined her. "There a problem here,

ladies?"

"No problem at all," Lizzie said. "Unless you count being mean-spirited a problem."

"Actually, I do." Jasper looked at Esther, and she went wide-eyed and embarrassed at being called out. Huffing, she turned and walked away from them.

"Thank you," Jasper said to Lizzie. "For defending Callie."

Lizzie sighed. "I wish I could do more. It won't be easy for her."

Those words were true. He hadn't realized until he'd seen it, the way so much of the town still saw her.

"Or for you," Lizzie said.

"Huh?"

Lizzie tilted her head to look up at him. "Ellie won't let her win, not without a fight. Be careful."

The warning took him by surprise. What was he to be careful of? "I surely will."

"Good," Lizzie answered by giving him an absent-minded pat on the arm. "I wouldn't trust Ellie as far as I could throw her. I believed that as a child, and I believe it now."

CHAPTER FOURTEEN

Callie

Now that her speech was done, Callie's heart ceased its rapid pounding and she felt herself calming. Before she'd taken to her speech, she'd been so nervous she'd nearly lost her breakfast out back of the clinic, but she'd never tell anyone.

As the crowd dispersed she shook the hands of a few people she'd never thought would approach her before.

"I liked your speech." Lizzie winked at her as she walked past with her husband.

That was something. If, as Lizzie had said, some members of the Women's Society were growing tired of Ellie, they might tell their husbands to vote the other way. Maybe, just maybe, she had a shot.

Callie went back to work. The saloon was full.

There had been a time when the only interaction Callie had had with the sheriff of Cricket Bend was to get an occasional warning about not wearing enough clothes when she sat on her balcony above the saloon. Those days were past, and she and Luke Anderson had developed a friendly relationship. Saloon owners needed to be on good terms with the lawmen in their town, as liquor had a funny way of turning the meekest of men into warriors, at least in their minds, and the slightest tease was suddenly a declaration of war worth brawling over.

After the speeches ended, after the crowd dispersed, Luke came to the saloon. He wasn't a drinking man, so Callie recognized it as a public show of throwing his hat into her ring as a candidate.

"You did good," Luke said.

"Thank you. Think I'll win?"

"He's got experience, but you've got a spark." Luke shrugged. "Just depends on which one the people want more. Either way, Cricket Bend will be all right. It'll take more than a mayor to destroy this town. I'll have a beer if you got one."

"I got a couple."

Luke looked around the saloon. "Looks like you got a good crowd."

"I didn't trip and fall on my face, or forget everything I was planning to say," she said. "I told them there'd be half-off drinks if I did a decent job."

"Don't sell yourself short. You did a real good job."

"You gonna vote for me?"

"I'm supposed to remain impartial."

"But you're here."

He winked at her. "Not sure if my opinion matters, but I want folks to know who I stand with."

He looked around the room at the drinking men, playing cards. "You've done a good job making this place something special."

"Hank did most of that—"

"Hank fixed it up so it wouldn't blow away with a big wind. You're the reason it's a success."

"Thanks, Luke. Just for that, your drink is on the house."

She saw Luke glance toward the table by the window, where Hank sat by himself. The man spilled out of the chair he was so big, and played a quick-handed game of what appeared to be solitaire.

"Why is Porter here?"

"There's poker," she said. "Where else would he be?"

"I mean in town."

"Whyn't you ask him?"

"Because if I get too close to him I might shoot him, and that's not good form for a man who's supposed to obey the law."

"I told him if he messed with Haven I'd kill him myself."

"I appreciate that," Luke said. He took a long drink.

"Luke?"

"You gonna let him be Nate's daddy?" Callie was surprised, and didn't answer. "You want my two cents, Callie girl?"

"I do indeed."

"Becoming a father don't take much," Luke said. "Everyone over the age of about thirteen knows how it happens. But it don't end there. A real man steps up and raises his child. He cares for him, he

137

wipes up the spit-up, he gets in there even when it's a messy, nasty business—and children, for all their sweetness, can be a messy, nasty business."

Callie laughed.

"But you do it because you love them. I would take a bullet for Haven any day of the week. Hell, I'd do it for Matthew too, and he ain't even my blood. And knowing that Porter is here, slithering around in the grass waiting to cause trouble, has me in mind to do some snake shooting."

"Don't shoot him here. Too many witnesses."

Luke wagged a finger in agreement.

"Funny, you're the second lawman in this town to talk about shooting him. Jasper said the same thing."

"Between us, I didn't used to think a whole lot of Jasper. I mainly only hired him originally because he was a friend of Matthew's. Thought he wasn't good for much more than drinking and carousing. But I was wrong. Since the moment Nate arrived on this earth, Jasper has been by your side and has been a father to that little boy."

"What are you saying, Luke?"

"You know what I'm saying. Seems to me you got a big choice to make—and if you choose wrong, I believe you will break Jasper's heart. Might even kill him. He loves that boy that much."

"He's a good man."

"And he loves you that much too."

"Luke."

"He loves you."

"Papa!"

Haven and Doc came into the saloon, ignoring

138

everyone as they strode toward Callie and Luke.

"Want a drink, Doc?" Callie asked.

Doc shook his head. "We got a problem."

Luke finished his shot. "We got a couple. Mind bein' more specific?"

"Carolee Fowler," Doc said.

"What about her? She hangs around the jail, but she ain't no trouble."

Doc looked at Haven and Callie. Haven winced and said, "She spent part of the morning hanging around the clinic like she wanted to come inside. She didn't, but she ducked around back at one point and was sick."

Callie's heart dropped. "Oh no."

Luke realized it too. "You think she's—"

Doc patted his belly a few times, and everyone caught his meaning. "I think she's in the kind of trouble that could lead to an all-out land war."

"Find Matthew and Jasper for me, would you?"

"What are you going to do?" Callie asked.

"I'm going to take Jeb Gorman back to his family," Luke said.

"Carolee's father and brothers will be furious at her," Callie answered.

"Maybe they should be."

"Maybe Jeb should share in the blame. A woman, a girl really, doesn't get pregnant all by herself. Shaming her won't help anything."

"What do you suggest we do?"

"I suggest you start by letting Jeb know he might be a daddy."

***

Jasper

"A daddy?" Jeb's hard expression melted as he sat down on the cot in the jail cell. Carolee stood at the bars of his cell, looking down at her nervously twisting fingers. Jasper was surprised by the news, but Jeb looked ready to faint. Behind Carolee stood a wall of people: Haven, Luke, Matthew, Callie, and Doc.

Carolee nodded. "Yes. I mean, I think so, at least. I been tired and eatin' everything I can get my hands on, and I've been sick most mornings. Those are signs, aren't they?" Carolee cast a look to the back of the room at Doc for his answer, and he nodded.

Jeb stared at the floor of the cell. "Were you gonna tell me?"

"I was trying to find a time to get to you," she said, sounding scared of what he would say next.

But Jeb got up from the bed and reached through the bars to link her fingers in his.

"Your daddies aren't going to like this," Luke said.

Jasper and Matthew exchanged a look. The real story behind the farmers' feud stood right in front of them, doe-eyed and swooning with young love.

Jeb stood up tall. "Well, they're going to have to live with it. We're gonna get married, like we said we would."

"That's what I hoped you'd say," Luke said. He turned to Jasper. "Bring the reverend here, would you?"

Reverend Carver came quickly, and walked into

the jail. He was a quiet man with a trim beard.

"Will you marry us right now?" Carolee asked when she saw him.

The reverend smiled. "I understand your eagerness. But I've known you both since you were children, and I know your fathers. I would prefer to do it with their permission."

"Papa won't approve," Carolee said.

The reverend stepped forward. "I will speak with him."

"I have sinned," she whispered.

He set a hand on her shoulder. "Don't bother judging yourself. Let him do that."

"Him and everyone else." She sighed.

The poor girl had a good point, unfortunately. Word would travel, and her reputation as a good girl would be ruined. Even if they got married that day, the baby would arrive early and folks would know. It would be a shame. Folks would call it a shotgun wedding, and no one would care if Carolee and Jeb truly cared for each other or not.

Jasper believed they did. As he watched, the two lovers held hand through the bars of Jeb's cell. Jeb bent down and kissed one of Carolee's fingers.

"We'll go out together," Luke said. "The boys, Jeb, you, the reverend, and me. See if we can't resolve this once and for all."

"Will you come with us?" Carolee grabbed Callie's hand.

"I better not," Callie said. "Ellie hates me enough."

"I'll go," Haven offered as she stepped to Carolee's side and put a hand on her back. Carolee gave her a smile of gratitude.

"I'm gonna let you out," Luke said. "And the first thing you will do is apologize to my deputy for that shiner you gave him. And then you will behave yourself."

"Yes, sir."

Jeb came out and stepped to Jasper. "I'm real sorry for what I done."

"I ain't mad," Jasper said. "You gotta grow up and be a man now." Funny how he was no more than three years older than Jeb. It felt like it was fifty.

"I aim to."

Luke, Jasper, Matthew, Haven, Carolee, Jeb, and Reverend Carver headed to the Fowler place. Carolee rode behind Jeb on a horse, her arms around the middle of the man she loved. About a mile out, Luke sent Matthew to round up the men and bring them to the contested fifty feet of land, the middle ground between the two ranches.

Jasper tied the horses to the fence posts.

"If things get ugly, duck behind me," Jasper said to the reverend.

The reverend smiled. "I'm hopeful it won't come to that."

"I'd like that too, believe me."

Haven pulled her shotgun from her saddlebag. She saw Jasper's raised eyebrow. "I'd prefer not to use it myself, but I'm not stupid enough not to plan for the worst."

Carolee and Jeb stood close together, holding hands.

"Poor kids," Luke said.

"What do we do?" Haven asked.

"We let Carolee and Jeb tell their fathers the truth, and hope that the reverend being here keeps things civil."

Men came riding fast. Carolee and Jeb turned to face them, hand-in-hand. The farmers jumped from their horses and charged forward, but Carolee said something and everyone stopped. The tension was too much, and Jasper stepped after the small group. Luke held a hand to his chest. "This ain't our business."

"It is if Sam Fowler goes after Jeb."

"It ain't easy being a father," Luke said. He looked at Haven, and Matthew who had joined them. "Believe you me. But Seth and Horace are good men under all their bluster. I have to believe they only want the best for their children. What's happening is happening, but I think they might just surprise you."

Horace Gorman and Sam Fowler looked aghast.

"They know," Haven said.

No one spoke, but they watched the scene play out, unable to hear what was being said. Luke was right; it was a family matter first and foremost. Jasper moved his hand to his pistol just in case someone jumped someone, and he noticed Matthew did the same.

And then Horace Gorman hugged Carolee.

And the reverend smiled and looked at the gathered group. One tiny nod was all he needed, and Luke, Jasper, Matthew, and Haven all released the breaths they'd been holding for too long.

Horace and Sam came to them.

"Sheriff," Fowler said. "Thank you for all you've done."

"My pleasure," Luke said. "Is this foolishness done?"

The fathers looked at each other and nodded. "It's done," Gorman said. "Reverend is going to marry them tomorrow, right on this piece of terrible soil."

"It's really bad soil," Fowler said. "Horace can have it."

"Hell, I don't want it."

"Whyn't you let them have it?" Matthew said with a smile. "And a little bit more on each side of it. They could build a place of their own."

"You know," Horace said. "That ain't a bad idea."

"I'm good like that sometimes."

"Shake on it," Luke said. "Before all of us."

They did, the two men actually smiling.

"The two of you, you did a good thing here. I'm proud to call you my friends."

Carolee and Jeb came over, Carolee going right to Haven. "Will you be there, when the baby comes?"

"Try and stop me," Haven said.

"Tell Callie I'm real grateful," Carolee said. "And tell her I hope she wins."

"Tell your soon-to-be husband to vote for her." Haven glanced at Jeb.

As Luke and his crew got on their horses to ride back to town, leaving the two families to come together as one, Jasper saw the way Jeb hooked his arm around Carolee's waist. The two lovers smiled at each other, eyes full of hope and stars.

They were too young, and the world had lots of challenges ahead for them.

But they had love.

That was a good enough start.

CHAPTER FIFTEEN

Callie

What she wouldn't have given to be able to be by Carolee's side for what was sure to be an ugly business, but it wasn't her place—and meddling in anything pertaining to Ellie Graham was sure to only bring trouble.

So she settled in on the steps outside of the saloon to play with Nate. The game he wanted to play involved his new train, a wooden horse that had previously been his favorite toy, and a lot of crashing the two together and whooping.

Simple things, the little moments she spent with her son, put things in focus. The fresh air soothed her, even with the dust the passing horses and wagons kicked up.

A woman cleared her throat.

Callie took a guess who it was.

"Ellie." Callie shifted herself and folded her arms, a posture of defiance to pretend that Ellie Graham standing just outside the saloon hadn't startled her. She indicated Nate. "This ain't the time for you and me to get started."

Ellie stared at her.

"Nate, honey, why don't you go inside? See if Hill has any peppermint."

Nate ran under the saloon doors.

Callie stood up on the step. "You best be sure your precious Women's Society doesn't catch sight of you standing here. Else they might decide to brand you a whore and turn their noses up at you."

Ellie took a step forward. "Your speech was good."

Callie put a hand to her chest. "Saints alive. Did you just pay me a compliment?"

"Don't get too excited," Ellie said. As she stepped closer, Callie saw her hard-set face. "Your speech won't matter, you know. Charles has had this election in the bag since before it even began. A man of his means and connections doesn't really need to go through getting elected, but he's a good man and insisted upon it."

"Is that so?" Callie asked. "From what I saw today, I might be giving him some competition."

Ellie smiled, and at the sight, Callie's heart sank. It was the smile of someone who knew something, had something up their sleeve, and was about to let it be known.

"You know, Mr. Knight at the newspaper owes me a couple favors. He'll run whatever I tell him on the front page—"

"Stop dancing around and tell me what you want." Callie's stomach felt upset.

"It's simple. Quit the election and leave Jasper alone, or I'm going to give him a list of all the men in town who visited you back when you were something considerably less than a respectable businesswoman."

"How do you know their names?"

"Women talk," Ellie said. "This town does love to gossip."

"That's all it would be, a list made of gossip."

"I have names and dates," she said. "A few women around these parts aren't happy their husband and beaus turned to sin."

Ellie was telling the truth; it was clear on her nasty face. Callie gulped. If the list got out, Callie would be ruined—for real and for good. She and Nate would have to leave Cricket Bend. She'd be unable to stand the shame of the faces of the men she'd kept quiet and confidential, the hallmark of a good upstairs girl.

She'd fought against her past every day for three years, hoping for a magical moment when those who looked down upon her would come to their senses and see who she really was.

Suddenly, Callie was done fighting. Spending every moment of all her days being up against something was too much. The taste of bile filled her mouth as she spoke. "Fine."

"Then we have an agreement."

"Yes," Callie said. "Though you should know Jasper won't give up that easy."

"He can get what you offer somewhere else."

"He loves me, you know."

Ellie was silent for a long moment. Her expression changed rapidly, but remained unreadable. "He's so much better than you," Ellie finally growled. Callie did not miss the wetness in the woman's eyes. She could almost, for once, bring herself to feel bad for Ellie. The woman was hurting deep down in the soul Callie hadn't known she'd had, and it was because of Jasper.

Callie moved closer to her, to spare her the embarrassment of passersby overhearing.

"I know he is," Callie replied. "That's why I told him to leave me be. I told him so many times."

"You did what?"

"Ellie, we both know that you relish talking about me every chance you get. You'd like to ruin me for good. Do that if you want. But I ain't about to let you ruin him. Hate me all you want, but leave him out of it."

"That's not why I hate you."

"I'm sure you got lots of reasons. I'm not interested in hearing them. Go home."

"How can a woman let men..." Ellie looked Callie up and down with disgust. "You must have unhappiness deep in your soul."

"It seems to me I'm not the unhappy one here."

"Ladies, is there a problem?"

Hank had come out the doors after Callie, and the sight of her and Ellie facing off had stopped him from advancing farther.

"I don't know." Callie raised an eyebrow to her foe. "Do we have a problem, Mrs. Graham?"

Ellie turned on her heel and flounced down the boardwalk. Callie started back inside, but Hank blocked her way. "What does that harpy want, coming here?"

"To tell me to quit the election and leave Jasper

alone."

"And you told her where she could shove it, though in uglier terms, I hope."

"I agreed."

"Callie!"

"I'm not sure it ain't a good idea. She's right. Charles probably has this election already won. I don't have a quarter of his money."

Hank looked mad. "Run for mayor or don't run for mayor. What about Jasper?"

"He and I—we ain't a good idea. I could only hurt him."

Hank scoffed. "Women. Always thinking you can turn men on and off like gas lamps. You could set fire to Jasper Tanner and he'd still stare at you with those big lovesick cow eyes of his." Back in the saloon he signaled to Ben, who poured a shot. Rather than drink it himself, Hank slid it over to her.

"I didn't think you paid attention to things like that."

"I pay attention to everything," Hank said. "It's the only reason I'm still alive."

Callie nodded, knowing his words to be truth. She went back behind the bar and picked up the rag to wipe down the carved wood at the far end of the bar, away from where Hill and Rip talked and drank. Hank followed her, staying on the other side of the bar.

"When I first got here, this bar was no more than four walls and two floors." He ran a hand over the polished wood counter. "The wind blew right through the cracks in the boards, and Hill and the boys were the only thing holding it up."

"I remember," she said. "The staircase used to shake when I went upstairs. Lucky it didn't collapse and kill me."

Hank smiled. "Seems like it was a hundred years ago."

"Sure does."

"Can I ask you something?"

"Like you're not going to anyway."

"Why does a woman push away a man who she loves, who loves her back just as much?"

"I can't explain it—"

"You're going to have to. Is it because of Braxton?"

That was it. She could handle no more. Between Ellie, and the election, and the thought of saying no to Jasper, and the very mention of Jack, Callie felt herself crumple. She felt her face twist and her eyes water and knew the emotions she'd been locking away weren't going to stay hidden anymore.

With a sound of fury, Callie swung her arm, sending a few glasses and a bottle flying to the ground with a smash. She hung onto the bar, but her knees bent, and she wept behind the bar.

"Jack," she whispered before the sobs came, great and overtaking.

Nate peeked around the corner. "Mama?"

Her son's little face was so concerned. "Oh, sweetie."

But she was not alone.

Hill was there in an instant by her side, taking the spilling bottle from the hand that still held it. Ed Dean reached for a cloth to wipe up the mess, and

Ben crouched by her side.

And then Hank was there.

And she was being lifted up by his arms and weeping into his shoulder and upstairs being set back on the bed instead of the floor. She fell face-down on the pillow and wailed.

Nate had followed, worried as a kid could be. "Mama?"

"Your mama is all right," Hank said in a kind tone. "She's just sad about something."

Nate kissed her cheek. "Don't be sad, Mama."

"Oh, sugar." Callie tried not to cry again, but there was no holding back.

Hill scooped Nate up. "Come on, buckaroo. Let's give your mama a little time. I'll take him for a walk down to Harper's. We'll get some rock candy."

"Find Jasper," Hank said.

"No," Callie refused. She didn't need him there. This grief needed to be with without Jasper's kindness. This was harder, built of a different time. Hank, she could handle. Jasper would have wrecked her.

Hill looked at Hank for approval, and Hank nodded.

Callie went back to burying her face, and everyone dispersed.

"I've known you for years, Callie, and I've never seen you shed one tear. I've seen you get mad and break things, and punch hard, but not one tear."

"Jack is dead," she confessed. Saying the words was such a relief.

"You're sure?"

"A doctor wrote me. He was killed in Tennessee by a man he was hunting."

"Damn," Hank whispered. "I never cared for him myself, but I know you did."

"I didn't know what had become of him."

"Would it have been better if he'd remained a mystery?" Hank wondered aloud. "So you could at least hope."

"Exactly."

Hank shrugged. "Life's funny that way. Not that this is funny. I don't mean that. But who would have thought we'd all be where we are right now? You and me, here like this. Yes, sir. Life is funny."

"I think I'll laugh tomorrow," she said.

He put am arm around her. She rested her head on his shoulder and let herself be held.

"I thought he'd run out."

"He wouldn't have."

"You did."

"Well, there's no accounting for me. But that man looked at you with love."

Callie took comfort in those words. She hadn't imagined it. Jack Braxton had cared for her, and maybe even loved her. But realizing that made her grief swell again, and she cried.

"Cry all you want," Hank said.

He smoothed her hair and held her close.

"I wasn't going to spend my life waiting on him, you know."

"That wouldn't be the Callie I know at all. She moves on."

"I did move on."

"But you didn't. You've been making yourself

miserable, and making Jasper miserable, because you haven't moved on."

"Why, Hank, do you give a damn about me?"

"I give a lot of damns about you." He looked at her with such honesty in his dark eyes, she even believed him. In the whole of their friendship, she hadn't been able to believe him many times. "If this is about your former profession—"

"Of course it's about that," she exclaimed. "What the hell else would it be?"

"Jasper knows better than anyone what you used to be."

"That's the problem."

"He's still here, isn't he? Fighting for you each and every day. You should be thrilled. Hell, he's fighting for you harder than Deputy Frank is—"

"Don't you butt into the Franks' business, Hank."

Hank held up a hand and shook his head. "I'm not. 'Least I'm trying not to."

"They will be fine. At least they would if you stopped getting in the way."

"I'm not—"

"I saw the pin on Haven's dress. I've never seen it before. It's too fancy to be from around here."

"I brought her a present."

"Stay away from her, and they'll be fine."

"Will they? Will you? I came back to Cricket Bend to find things have fallen all to hell. You stand on the brink of having the kind of life most folks dream about, and you're scared of what, Ellie Graham? To hell with her. She's a jealous toad dressed in expensive petticoats."

154

"You're a funny man," Callie said. "When you're not being a useless rogue."

Hank nodded. "I've been called worse."

Callie looked long and hard at him. Getting Jasper to leave her be might be a bigger problem. The man loved her, confessed it openly, and wasn't the kind to go running at trouble. He'd stand and fight, unfortunately.

Unless Callie played a hand she'd not previously thought of.

A tall, dark, handsome hand who sat up against her, looking like a well-dressed dream.

"I have an idea," Callie said. "But I'm gonna need your help."

Hank put a hand on his heart and fake wobbled. "Knock me down with a feather, Miss Callie. Did you just say what I think you said?"

"It's a good thing you're good-looking," she bit back. "'Cause you're sure a pain in the ass more often than not."

"Which of my services do you require?"

Callie gulped. "The one you're best at."

Hank raised an eyebrow at her. "Right here and now? I should lock the door."

"I meant deception."

"Ouch," Hank said, standing up. "That cuts me deep, beautiful."

Something about her manner must have alerted Hank that something more than minor was happening, for all teasing dropped away from him and he stood over her. "What's this plan?"

"I'm laying out all my cards, Hank. Don't you think it'd be better, for the ones we love the most I mean, if you and I were seen as being together?"

"You've lost your mind."

"Jasper asked me to marry him."

"Did you say yes?"

"No."

"Why not?"

She gave him a look. "Do I really need to explain to you of all people why a lawman and a former whore shouldn't get married?"

"If you're worried about people talking about you, they already do."

"And that's fine, but if I can keep them from talking about him in the same way I'll take it."

"He won't care."

"He will when a list of all my former clients winds up on the front page of the paper and he can't look a man in town in the eye anymore."

"Ellie has that list?"

"So she says," Callie answered. "I love Cricket Bend. I want to raise Nate here. And I can't do that if she lets it out. And also, if you hadn't noticed, your returning to town has made things hard on Matthew and Haven. Harder than they already were, I mean. Let's take ourselves out of the game, Hank."

"You'll never win the election if you're with me."

"I'm not going to win anyway. Charles Graham had it locked down months ago. He's got more money than God and a shrew of a wife who'll claw the eyes out of anything that gets in her way." Callie fell back on the bed.

"So we'd pretend to be together."

"We don't need to pretend, if you want it that way." Callie shrugged. What difference would it make?

Hank didn't respond to the insinuation. "This seems like the kind of move that sends souls on a path to Hell."

"We're both headed straight for Hell anyway. We might as well go together."

"The Jezebel and the Scoundrel."

"The way it used to be." Callie's heart gave a thud in her chest at the memories. Her old life had been wild, full of sin and celebration, but underneath the loud laughter and at the bottom of all the bottles, she'd never found more than sadness.

All she'd wanted was home.

Home was in her grasp now, and she was too scared to take a hold of it.

"You don't want this," Hank whispered as he sat beside her on the bed.

"What I want doesn't matter."

"Haven said that to me once," he said quietly.

"Forget her," Callie said. "For her sake. And I'll forget Jasper for his."

Hank fell back on the bed beside her. "If this is what you want, I will play along."

What she wanted was Jasper, his sweetness and his kisses, to be a part of her every day. But to think it could ever be, she'd been naïve and foolish. Hank wasn't the kind of man to hang your life on, but Callie saw no other solution.

"Haven is supposed to come by in the morning with the posters. We might as well start tomorrow."

"What do you want me to do?"

"You didn't happen to bring that red dress with you, did you?"

CHAPTER SIXTEEN

Jasper

Waking up without worrying if today was the day he'd have to arrest two-dozen farmers, or haul their dead bodies to the undertaker, was a nice feeling. Jasper woke in his own bed, started some water boiling for coffee, and went out on the porch.

The rope swing blew in the breeze.

One situation was resolved. It was time to handle the other, this time for real.

He went to town, ready to draw a line in the sand with Callie. Either she would marry him or she wouldn't. That would be that, and the matter would be done.

Haven wasn't a tall woman, and she carried a stack of posters about a quarter of her height high as she made her way to the saloon. Jasper half-smiled. Nothing could ever hold Haven Frank down for long. Since he'd wanted an excuse to see Callie anyway, helping with the posters seemed finely timed.

"Let me carry those." Jasper scooted up to Haven

and took the pile of posters from her arms.

"I can manage," she said.

"I know," he said. "But let me take some and at least pretend to be a gentleman, would you?"

"Fine," she said with a smile. "Thank you kindly, Mr. Tanner."

"You're welcome, Mrs. Frank. Where's Matthew today?"

"He's somewhere," she said, and left it at that.

There was trouble in the Frank house; Jasper knew it for sure when he saw the distant look in Haven's eyes at the mention of her husband. Haven and Matthew had exemplified love for as long as he could remember, so to think of them falling apart gave a man a feeling of hopelessness. If they couldn't make it, who the hell could?

"Nate's turning three in a couple weeks," Jasper offered. "Callie was thinking we should have a party."

"We should," Haven agreed. "He's such a darling little boy. And who knows, a few weeks from now maybe we'll soon be celebrating the new mayor of Cricket Bend." Haven actually laughed, a sound Jasper liked to hear.

"Here's hoping," Jasper replied. He pushed open the saloon door so she could pass through, and nearly ran right into the back of her as she'd stopped dead in her tracks.

On the steps of the saloon, first thing in the morning, Callie and Hank were kissing.

It was no sweet little kiss either. Callie leaned against the support beam, and Hank surrounded her and rested his hand on her waist. It looked convincing.

Furthermore, Callie was dressed to kill. She wore a red dress, cut high to show off her shapely legs, and cut low on top to show the tops of her bosoms. The dress was sex, and suggested an entirely different woman. Her blonde hair was down, falling over her bare shoulders.

Jasper felt charged with desire for her and yearned for murder and revenge on Hank Porter all in that moment. The bastard had come back to town for one reason and one reason only, and it was to take away the things Jasper most prized. Well, he'd have a hell of a fight first.

Haven let the posters in her hands fall to the ground. They fluttered before they landed.

Callie and Hank broke their kiss, and looked down at the two shocked faces.

"Oh my," Callie said with surprise.

Jasper saw through the charade immediately. He knew Callie's surprised face when she was being honest. He'd seen it a hundred times, had seen it in the moonlight the other night when she'd kissed him and liked it.

They'd been meant to see the display, both he and Haven.

For what reason he didn't know, but he decided to play along. "Good morning."

"Morning," Hank said, his eyes never leaving Haven's. Haven tensed, all the light that had been in her eyes only a few moments earlier gone and dark again. Yet another reason Jasper wanted to punch Hank Porter in the jaw.

"What are you doing?" Jasper asked Callie.

The Callie he loved vanished, and the Callie who worked on flash and sparkle returned. "Why, darlin', what does it look like I'm doing?"

"It looks like you're taking up with a scoundrel."

"I'll try not to take offense at that," Hank said.

"I meant you offense. A whole lot of it."

"Now hold on a minute." Callie frowned.

Jasper shook his head. "All this looks to me like you're taking up with him again. But I know you're not that stupid."

"Jasper—" Haven grabbed hold of his arm. "Let's go."

"You go," he said. "Get as far away from here and the two of them as you can. Me, I'm not going anywhere."

"We're getting married," Callie announced.

Haven's grip on Jasper's arm grew tighter. He barely felt it.

"Being that Hank is Nate's daddy, and knows more about running saloons than anyone in the world, we figured it'd be best for everyone if we made it official. We're going to be wed on Saturday at sunset. We'd love for you both to come."

"You're lying," Haven said.

"I wouldn't lie about something so important." Callie pointed to the posters. "And, I'm dropping out of the election."

"What?" Haven found her voice, firm and furious.

"Charles Graham would be a better mayor, and he's gonna win anyway. I don't know why I've been putting myself through so much hell thinking I had a chance. He'll win, and I'm going to run this place, and that's that."

Callie stepped down the stairs and aimed herself toward Haven. It was her, in the flesh, but it wasn't. The woman who spoke to them, and said such confusing things, was playacting in a costume she didn't belong in anymore.

There was real fear in Callie's eyes when she reached Haven. "I hope you're not upset with me."

Haven stepped backward. "Let's go," she whispered, still holding Jasper's arm in near desperation. She looked ready to collapse. He wasn't sure he wouldn't do the same himself.

Without answering Callie's invitation or so much as a word, Jasper turned and left the saloon with Haven in tow. Her breathing grew ragged, and she seemed about ready to shatter into pieces. He put an arm around her and whisked her into the empty clinic.

Once inside, Haven went to the counter and put her hands down. She breathed out.

"You all right?"

"Are you?"

"Nope."

"I can't believe her," Haven said. "Callie is not stupid, and that—" Haven pointed in the direction of the saloon. "That is the stupidest damn move I have ever seen, and believe me I know stupid moves when I see them."

Jasper nodded.

"To think I actually thought he'd come here to be a better man." Haven reached for her dress and pulled a pin off, then threw it on the ground. It rolled under the hospital bed and she didn't go after it.

"What was that?"

"My stupidity. I'm a damned fool, Jasper."

"You and me both."

"I'm not surprising you when I tell you it's you she's crazy about, am I?"

"Actually, you are."

"Come off it, Jasper," Haven said. "The two of you have been crazy about each other for years now. You're crazy for her, and she's the same, and now she's done this and it doesn't make a lick of sense."

"She did it for me," Jasper said. "And for you."

"What?"

"I don't know what happened between you and Hank."

"Stupidity, like I said, but nothing of consequence."

"I don't know if that's true. If it was, you wouldn't be this upset."

"I am upset with my best friend acting like a lunatic."

"If she'd been kissing any other man, would you be this upset?"

Haven went silent.

"Go home to Matthew."

"Jasper—"

"I know we're not really friends. Hell, we might never be friends, but I need you to trust me. Go home to him."

"What are you going to do?"

"I'll handle it."

Haven bit her lip. "Doc'll be back shortly, and

I'll head home once he is. Matthew's there right now. He's fixing the roof."

"Go to him," Jasper pleaded. "Forget Hank Porter for good. Go to the man who loves you enough to die for you. Whatever is going on with the two of you, fix it. Fix it because I don't know if I can fix the rest of this, and I need to know something will be good in the end."

CHAPTER SEVENTEEN

After a terrible two days of rolling what he'd seen and heard and said around in his mind like a wheel, Jasper looked forward to a night shift at the jail. With his position, there'd been no avoiding seeing Callie and Hank around town. They walked arm-in-arm, and anyone who hadn't known better would have believed their charade.

The town was quiet. Maybe he'd have some time to think. Maybe he didn't want to.

"There's a problem."

He looked up with a start to see Hill peeking his head into the jail.

"Of course there is," Jasper said.

He followed Hill across the street into the saloon.

What he saw happening inside made his jaw drop. Matthew stood at the bar. The normally tall-standing man leaned and swayed a bit as he laughed and shouted overtop everyone else.

Matthew was drunk. There was no missing it.

In all the years Jasper had been his friend, he'd

seen Matthew drink only a few times, and never to excess. He looked around the room and saw many familiar faces, but Callie was nowhere to be seen. Not that he wanted to see her, of course.

Hill stepped beside Jasper. "He's been like that for nearly an hour now. I told him to get going home, but he nearly slugged me."

"Thanks, Hill," Jasper said. "I'll take care of him."

Unfortunately, Hank came through the crowd and reached Matthew first. The bigger man had discarded his tailored jacket for the evening, and wore a vest and shirtsleeves. There was no mistaking the strength of him, or the fact that Hank could throw Matthew out fairly easily in his current state.

"You've had enough, Deputy." Hank set a hand on Matthew's arm.

Matthew flung his hand off. "Don't you touch me. I am enjoying myself."

Hank held up his hands. "You're drunk and disorderly. You'd throw out a man in your condition. You know it's the truth."

"You ain't throwing me out."

"Nope." Jasper jumped in before things got mean. "But I am."

Matthew hadn't noticed he was there before, obviously. There was such an expression of shame and surprise on his face, Jasper recognized his friend at last.

"Hey, brother. You want a drink?"

"Come on. Let's get some coffee in you and get you home to Haven."

"Maybe there ain't a point," Matthew said. "Maybe she'd rather be with him."

Matthew reached into his pocket and pulled something out, then slammed it onto the bar.

When he pulled his hand away, Jasper saw a small pin in the shape of a purple flower.

"I think this belongs to you," Matthew said. "Thought I'd bring it back."

Hank smirked. "Pretty, isn't it? Bluebonnets bring back such sweet memories for me."

Matthew clenched his fists.

"This ain't the time to do this," Jasper said. "Come on." He grabbed Matthew's arm.

Matthew shoved him. Jasper stumbled back a few steps, then collected himself in time to see Matthew move closer to Hank. "You came back here for her, don't deny it."

"I won't," Hank said.

Matthew nodded. "You—and Callie—you made her cry. I've never really understood what it is, what brings her here and draws her to you two, but it made her cry today. She came home, and she tried not to show it, but I saw it. I know every damn look that ever crosses her face, and I know when she's been crying. So maybe the best thing I can do for all involved is to drink the rest of that bottle and drown. I'll be out of your way."

"Self-pity does not become you." Hank took the bottle Matthew had been drinking from, and handed it back toward the bartender.

Matthew reached for it, but Jasper put himself in between the men. "Come on, Matthew."

"Nope."

168

"I'll go get Luke if you want." Jasper hated to threaten to tattle, but nothing would bring Matthew around like the idea of Luke getting involved.

Appearing behind the bar, Callie spoke up. "I'll handle this, Jasper."

"You handled enough," Jasper said, glaring at her.

"Matthew, honey—" Callie tried.

"Don't call me that," Matthew spit. "Did you invite him here?"

"What?"

"Was this your plan—to break two men's hearts in one swoop?" Matthew looked at Jasper. "'Cause well done, if that was the plan. It sure as hell worked." He took the gun from his belt and pushed it across the bar to her. "Might as well shoot me down right here."

At the sound of Matthew's voice, hearing the man sound beyond broken, Jasper had had enough. He grabbed Matthew by both arms and turned him toward the door of the saloon. They were nearly outside, nearly free of the place, when Hank's voice came.

"Matthew," Hank called.

Matthew turned half-around in the doorway.

"If you don't fight for her, you're a fool."

"If it was as easy as fighting you, I'd agree."

"You've never really fought me," Hank said.

"I'm willing to, you son of a bitch."

"Boys," Callie warned.

Hank pulled his gun from his own belt and set it on the bar. Jasper was grateful to see that. If they were going to kill each other, they'd need to use their hands. It would take longer, and would give him more time to figure out how to put a stop to it.

Matthew lunged for Hank, and Hank avoided the punch and pushed Matthew out the doors of the saloon, following him out onto the boardwalk. Matthew swung again, and the two men fell as one down the five steps to the street.

Callie and Jasper stood, gaping. Men from the saloon came out to watch as well.

They rose to their feet, two men squaring off over a long-held grudge.

"There any point in trying to stop them?" Callie asked.

Jasper shook his head. "Why do you care?"

"I don't want Matthew to get hurt."

Not even the look of utter surprise on her face could stop Jasper from growling at her. "If you think Hank is the kind of man who would hurt a drunk, it makes me wonder why you'd align yourself with him."

"He's not—"

"And why you'd put Nate in that position." Jasper held up a hand. "Right now this ain't about you and me, and it ain't even about Nate. Matthew is my best friend, and I need to stop him before he winds up dead or in jail."

"You think he'd kill Hank?"

"I think he'd take the chance if he saw it. And I think I know how he feels. Shit, Callie, you were better off with Braxton than Hank."

"Braxton is dead."

He spun on her.

"I didn't tell anyone. Everyone was so hopeful."

She looked at the dirt. "I suppose all that hope is gone now, anyway."

Of all the terrible timing, Jasper thought. No wonder she'd been so determined to hold herself back. Losing someone that way could make anyone build a wall around their heart.

"You should have told me."

"It wouldn't have made any difference," she said. "We're not supposed to be, you and I."

"Goddammit, Porter!"

Out for blood, Matthew held nothing back. Jasper tore his attention back to the men, and stepped down the stairs to the fight. He called to Matthew a few times, but Matthew didn't seem to hear—his eyes were cold and, though Hank had a broader build and more bulk, Matthew had the fire of hatred on his side. For his part, Hank took a defensive stance—as if he wanted to stop Matthew from killing him, but didn't especially mean the younger man harm.

Until something changed. After only a minute, Hank hunkered down and started to swing back. His bloody mouth grimaced as he landed a square punch on Matthew's nose and sent him nearly to the ground.

"Goddammit," Jasper called. "Stop it!"

Neither stopped. Neither even hesitated.

Jasper charged into the fight, but was taken by surprise when both men shoved him back out.

"Hank!" Callie yelled. "If you so much as take one more swing, I will never speak to you again."

"They're gonna kill each other," Hill hollered.

Jasper knew it was the truth. Things were

escalating quicker than he'd thought. For being drunk, Matthew was full of rage and able to bounce back after getting hit. He didn't go down, no matter how many hits he took. The brawl continued on. Hank threw Matthew onto the steps of the saloon, but Matthew got back up and landed another punch on Hank's strong jaw. They grunted and bled like two animals fighting to the death.

What would Luke do? Jasper reached for his gun, remembering the way Luke had stopped the farmer brawl with a warning shot into the air.

Before he could fire, the crack of a gunshot was heard.

Everyone jumped. Hank and Matthew stopped fighting, frozen with Hank pulled back ready to punch Matthew, who he held by the shirt, in the face. Matthew looked beaten, ready to fall.

Jasper turned to see who had fired.

"Jeepers," Callie breathed.

Haven stood in the street a distance back from everyone. She wore a duster over a white nightgown, and her long dark curls were loose. Most notably, she held her shotgun in her hands, aimed high at the sky overtop the town.

"What are you doing here?" Matthew grumbled.

"I came looking for my husband, who didn't come home," she called.

The two men glared at each other. Matthew started to move, but Haven spoke and stopped him. "The next one of you who moves, I will shoot in the leg. And I won't patch you up afterward." She lowered the gun slightly.

At the sight of her, Hank struck a final blow and

sent Matthew to the ground.

He turned to Haven, eyes hard on her, as if challenging her resolve.

She cocked the gun again and aimed it at him.

Jasper saw that she was trembling.

No one moved.

Hank stood over Matthew. The scoundrel was bleeding from his nose and his shirt was torn, but he didn't look away from Haven. At his feet, Matthew groaned, but made no attempt to get up.

"Get out of here," Haven finally said. Never had Jasper heard any voice as icy.

"Or what?" Hank replied.

"Or I'll shoot you like I should have shot you two years ago."

"You don't mean that."

Hank held up his hand, and tossed something to her. Jasper saw a small flash of light reflected as it flew through the air. Haven caught it easily and looked at it for a second.

Then she dropped it into the dirt.

"If you were going to shoot me, you would have done it."

Haven fired a shot. Hank jumped, but she'd fired just over his shoulder on purpose. If Jasper hadn't been wound so tense, he would have chuckled at her pluck. Being the daughter of the sheriff and the wife of a deputy, she knew her way around a gun.

"You feel like testing me again? Get away from my husband."

Hank frowned, turned on his heel, and went off down the street into the darkness of the night. Once he was out of sight, Haven lowered her gun to her side, and exhaled for what seemed like five minutes. Her head fell back, and she shook it as she looked up at the stars.

Then, she looked at Jasper.

"Can you help me with him?"

"Come on, boys," Callie called out. "Round of drinks on me."

Nothing made men move faster than free libations, and the street cleared in moments. Callie followed the throng of men into the saloon like a dog herding sheep. As she went inside she looked back to them—himself, Haven, and Matthew, three of her closest friends, as if she was leaving them behind forever.

Maybe she was. At that moment, Jasper didn't particularly care.

Matthew raised himself up on his arms and got his knees underneath him. Jasper rushed to his side, meeting Haven on the ground.

"I don't think that will improve your standing with the Women's Society," Jasper quipped.

"I don't think it could get much worse." Haven dropped her gun and reached for Matthew's face. "Let me see."

Matthew lifted his head. Between the blood and the swelling, no one who didn't know him would have ever guessed the man was good-looking.

"Oh, Matthew." Haven touched the bridge of his nose. "Does that hurt?" Matthew shook his head. "This?" He shook his head again. Haven checked him all over, touching each part of him and waiting for a call of pain, but none came.

"Nothing's broken," he said.

"That's a blessing." Haven sighed. "Are you done with this now?"

"Are you done with him?"

The third wheel, Jasper held his breath. If the two of them couldn't find a way past their problems, what hope did anyone else in the world have?

"I've been done with Hank since the day I married you."

"You've been happier since he came back."

Haven shook her head. "He reminds me of better times, that's all. I look at him and I remember not being so sad all the time." She touched Matthew's cheek with such tenderness, his eyes closed and he bent into her fingers. Haven looked to Jasper. "Help me get him over to the clinic."

"I'm fine."

"You're bleeding from a few places," she said. "I'm going to clean you up before you get an infection. That's the last thing we need."

Matthew groaned. "If Doc sees me, he's going to tell Luke."

"You haven't seen yourself," Jasper answered. "No one's gonna miss that you were in a fight." He hooked Matthew under the arm, and Haven took the other side, and they helped him up off the ground. In the clinic, Haven washed the cuts and bandaged them, and put cool cloths on the places where bruises were most likely to form.

While he was glad to see her so attentive to Matthew, he remembered Callie's words.

Braxton was dead.

Holy hellfire, but that explained some things.

How long had she known, and had it wrecked her? Had she wept for him in secret, alone with her pain? The thought of Callie hurting that way punched him right in the heart.

"Jasper?" Haven asked. "Where are you?"

"I'm right here."

"You're somewhere else," she said. "You've been looking at that wall for a few minutes."

"Callie said Braxton is dead."

Matthew turned to him. "I never heard nothing about that."

"She didn't tell us. We were all too hopeful."

"And she didn't want to ruin it, of course. Poor Callie." Haven shook her head.

Matthew sighed. "I'll tell Luke first thing tomorrow." He tried to stand up, but groaned.

"Will he be all right?" Jasper asked.

Haven turned her eyes to her husband. "We will be all right."

CHAPTER EIGHTEEN

Hank

In a man's life, there came a few moments when he realized he'd chosen from two paths and could never go back again. No matter his wish, his desire, the beauty of hindsight, or any number of prayers, there was no going back. There'd been that moment, when Haven had stood there with her shotgun, just before Hank had slugged Matthew to that ground that last time, when he could have gone another way. Rather than throwing that punch he could have backed away and gone into the saloon and drank more and drowned out the vision of the yellow-haired man whose life he'd shattered by walking back into town.

What the hell had Matthew Frank ever done to him?

Nothing, if he was being honest.

All Matthew Frank had ever done was love Haven.

By hurting him, Hank had only really hurt

177

himself.

She had dropped the pin—and their past—into the dust.

He stormed to the livery, not sure entirely where he was going, but not certain stealing a horse and running wouldn't be the best solution. There was safety in the dark stable, where no one was around to see him drop any and all acts and be alone in his pain. Looking down at himself, he remembered each blow he'd struck. His shirt was torn, three buttons missing from the front, and there were drops of blood on his pants.

His nose had bled. He wiped it away with the sleeve of his destroyed shirt.

Everything had been destroyed. In Haven's eyes now, he was less than dirt. He couldn't live in the same city and breathe the same air as her, knowing that.

Roaring in fury, Hank pushed over a barrel. It fell with a thump and rolled a bit until it landed in front of a pair of heeled boots.

For a second, Hank thought the boots were Haven's. Perhaps he'd been entirely wrong. Perhaps she'd come after him and they'd run away from—

"That was sure something."

The boots did not belong to Haven.

It took a rascal to know one, and Hank knew Ellie Graham before he saw her.

"Forgive me. I am not in the mood for conversation, Mrs. Graham."

"I should think not. From the way you fought, and the way you walked away from Haven and her gun, I'd say you were in a different kind of mood

178

entirely."

Women had looked at Hank the way Ellie looked at him countless times before. Cornering him in a dark livery wasn't a move she'd made by mistake.

"You could have killed Matthew."

"Easily."

Ellie stepped forward to cross the distance between them. "And you didn't. Why?"

"There would have been no good outcome for me."

"It was calculated, then?"

He hadn't been thinking clearly enough to calculate. If he had, he'd have never started into the fight, never let Matthew's words get under his skin. "There didn't appear to be time for calculation."

She smiled. It reminded Hank of a fox.

"You're an interesting man," she said. "A paradox, I think. On one hand, you have a reputation not to be envied. On the other hand, not one but two women in this town—smart women too—seem willing to throw away good men for you."

Ellie didn't have her facts straight, but Hank wasn't going to argue.

Especially when she reached out a hand and set it on the bare skin on his chest where his shirt was open. "I admit, I'm curious to know what the allure is."

Hank saw her plan before she began it. He was out of sorts to be sure, but he wasn't absent of all his senses. Ellie Graham was making a move to seduce him.

"I think we're alike, Mr. Porter."

"I think you're in over your head, Mrs. Graham."

"Am I?"

She kissed him, a hard push of lips against his. She had to rise up on her tiptoes to do it, but Hank didn't discourage it. She was real and breathing and, if he was being honest, appealing enough of a woman with her good figure and the hunger with which she kissed him and clutched his shirt. His body stirred in response.

He'd lost himself in women before, many times. There was no better way for a man to lose himself, he figured. They were alone in the barn and it was late. He could have done anything, and she'd have let it happen. He could take it all out on her—his anger, his broken heart, his jealousy—and she'd not have stopped him. He could have closed his eyes and bent her over and pretended she was Haven, and no one would have been the wiser.

Ellie's hands slid down to his pants, and she started to unbuckle his belt. He grunted as she fumbled for him. Breaking her lips from his, Ellie whispered, "Do you want to forget her? Forget them all?"

Speechless, Hank bent his head down and landed his lips on her shoulder.

Ellie's hands went to the buttons of her dress, making quick work of them. She all but tore her dress open, and just before she revealed herself, he found the strength to stop her by taking her hands in his.

Under any other circumstances, he'd have taken her up on her scheme. But he'd done this—he and Callie, together. They'd done a stupid thing, and now he faced the consequences.

"Mrs. Graham, stop."

"What is the problem?"

"I won't be your revenge," he said.

"What if I'm yours?" Ellie looked up at him, and gave him a wicked look as she opened her bodice for him.

He looked. He couldn't not look, and liked what he saw, but quickly looked away and rubbed his hand over his face. "I am flattered, Mrs. Graham, but I believe you have the wrong impression of me."

"I'm pretty sure I have the perfect impression."

"I don't fool with married women."

"We both know that's just because the one you want won't let you."

His jaw set hard at those words, and he stepped back away from her.

Ellie chuckled, and buttoned her dress back up. "Is this where you pretend to be noble?"

"This is where I avoid getting caught up in a spider's web. I've enough trouble on my own. Good night, Mrs. Graham. I trust no one will ever know what transpired here."

"Not unless you say something." Ellie shrugged, as if trying to pretend she wasn't bothered by the encounter. "Think how easily I could spin this so you come out looking worse than you already do." Her eyes got wide and fluttery, and her voice breathy. "Oh, Sheriff Anderson. Thank goodness I found you. It's Hank Porter. The rascal came out of nowhere and grabbed me."

"He wouldn't believe you."

"He had this on him."

Ellie held up the pin.

She must have dug it out in the aftermath of the fight. It was his, indeed. Many people would attest to it. Ellie was just like him: used to getting what she wanted, and furious when it didn't go her way. But she had a card to play, in that Sheriff Anderson and everyone else in town would now think him the scoundrel he'd always been rumored to be.

She had the upper hand. Not only on Callie with her foul list of clients, but on him as well.

"Not a word," he said.

She left the barn.

"Sweet Father Christmas," Hank whispered. He dropped down onto a bale of hay and put his hands on his face. He needed a shave, but there wasn't time to think about grooming.

The real danger in Cricket Bend wasn't him at all. It was packaged in finery and influence, a seething pile of jealousy. Ellie prickled like a spark ready to ignite, and it was the kind of madness that made people do stupid things.

He couldn't win back Haven's affections, but he could at least keep Callie safe.

CHAPTER NINETEEN

Jasper

"Miss Lee." Jasper kept his words formal and his posture tall. He'd come to the saloon on that Sunday morning knowing full well most of the town would be over at the church. There'd be less people around to interfere. Only a few people—likely just Ben and Hill—would see how scared he was and how much he didn't want to do what he was about to do. "I need you over at the jail."

"For what?"

"Gotta file a report about what happened," he said. "And no one's seen head or tail of Hank since he stormed off, so you're the most reliable witness."

"You were there same as me."

"I'm deputy. I don't count in this."

Callie sighed loudly. "Keep an eye on Nate?" Callie asked of Ben and Hill.

He led her to the jail. Neither spoke on the way.

Jasper stepped in and closed the door behind them. He went around to the chair and sat, and pulled out a pad of paper. "Now tell me what happened."

"You know damn well what happened. Matthew got drunk and Hank beat the tar out of him until Haven nearly killed them both."

"I don't mean between Matthew and Hank."

"You don't?"

"I mean you're gonna tell me why you never told anyone about Braxton, and what the hell happened that made you quit the election and play as if you and Hank were a thing again." Jasper leaned back in the chair and put his feet up. "I've gone over it and over it in my head these past few days, and it don't add up."

"It is none of your business." She turned to go.

"You walk out that door, I'll arrest you for being uncooperative."

Her eyes flared. "I dare you to try it."

He leaned forward in his chair. "I'll do it."

Without taking her eyes from his, she took a step toward the door. Jasper jumped up from the chair and blocked her way. She struggled a bit, but he flung her over his shoulder and carried her over to the cell, plopped her down on the bed, and fled out, locking the door just before she could chase him.

"Let me out," she demanded.

"Nope."

"Luke will fire you for this."

Jasper shrugged. "I doubt it. I done dumber things and he ain't fired me yet."

He slipped the keys into the pocket of his pants and went back to his chair, putting his feet back on the desk.

Callie did a full circle, looking at every part of the cell. "You locked me up."

"I sure did."

"You bastard."

"Do I have your attention now?"

"You have my full attention, Deputy."

"All right then. What the hell did you think you and Hank would accomplish?"

"You locked me up 'cause of that?"

"Way I see it, you're out of your mind and apt to cause yourself harm. I locked you up for your own good. You ain't getting out of there until you tell me the truth, so you might want to start talking. I'd be happy to arrange for Nate to spend the night at Doc's, if this goes long."

"I'm not yours," she said.

"Maybe you should be."

They stared at each other like two people before a shootout. Jasper held strong, jaw set hard, eyes focused. Callie did the same.

More than a minute passed in stubborn silence before Callie growled in annoyance and went to sit down on the cot with a furious flop. "I hate you."

"Sure," he answered.

"This isn't fair."

"Don't talk to me about fair. You left me hanging without explaining a thing."

"It was my hope that I could end some things," she said, "Start some new things." Suddenly she got angry and folded her arms. "I don't owe you answers. Except to say that I'm the stupidest woman to ever walk the earth."

"Hardly the stupidest," Jasper replied. "Though,

to be fair, that was a real dumb plan."

"I know," she answered. "I'm in a jail cell. Haven's furious at me. Luke's disappointed. And Matthew and Hank…Lord have mercy, no one's seen him since the fight. Is Matthew hurt bad?"

"He's gonna look terrible for a week or so, but he's fine."

"I'm sorry he got hurt," she said. "And, for what it's worth, I'm sorry you got hurt too."

"Why did you do it?" he asked. "Did you think for a second that I'd buy it?"

"I guess I hoped you would," she said.

The way she looked down at the floor instead of into his eyes killed him. There was something Callie didn't want to say to him, and he couldn't go another minute without knowing it. "I know I scared you when I asked you to marry me," he said. "Hard to miss that, the way you ran off."

"I—"

"If you don't want to marry me, you can just tell me. There's no need to go to such trouble. I know you were holding out hope Braxton would come back—"

"It's not that I don't want to marry you," she replied, too forcefully.

"Then what is it? What in the world is keeping us apart when, for the life of me, I can't think of one good reason we shouldn't get married right this second? Or, rather, I can think of a reason but I pray to God it ain't the one. Do you love me at all, Callie?"

Disbelief. That was all he saw on her face. "I love you more than you know."

"Then what on earth are we standing here for? Marry me."

"I can't—"

"Why not?"

"In the eyes of this town I am a ruined woman. I will not ruin you."

There it was: the truth he'd waited to hear. He'd long suspected part of the problem causing her delay had to do with her former profession, but hearing it spoken aloud made him fill with anger. He rose from his chair and walked to the cell bars.

"You listen to me, and you listen good. I love you. I don't care what you used to do, or what people think of you for it. You're beautiful and funny and smart and impossible and I love you so much it feels like I could fly when you're near me. Don't you ever say that again, that you're ruined. It ain't true."

"Jasper—"

"You want to talk about shame? I spent an awful lot of time fooling around with Ellie, and it didn't stop just because she got married. And I didn't do it in order to keep myself alive and fed. I did it because I was young and hot-blooded and dumb enough to let my manhood do the thinking instead of my brain."

"She told me to stay away from you," Callie blurted. "Or she'd spread a list of all the men I…"

"She did, did she?" Jasper asked.

Callie nodded.

From his pocket, Jasper pulled the ring of keys. He unlocked the cell door. "Well, that's that then. She don't have the right to do such a thing—and she can't do a thing that'll keep me away from you."

He opened the door to the cell.

Callie didn't make a move to step out. "I won't ruin you."

"You already have. In the best way of all ways."

"I love you, Jasper."

And in a flash, Callie was flying from the cell and her sweet arms were around him again. She clutched him close, and he held her right back. Tears fell from her eyes and she kissed him hard and strong. Jasper's heart could have exploded right then and there.

The kisses grew in intensity. Their breathing grew faster.

He lifted her up and carried her over to Luke's desk and set her down on it.

"Here and now?" Callie giggled as her eyes darted to the cells.

Jasper smiled. "Not here and now. The next time I make love to you, there'll be flowers and wine and you'll not doubt I mean it to be forever."

"I bet I could convince you otherwise."

"I'm sure you could," he answered. "But I'm prepared."

He dropped to a knee.

"Jeepers," she breathed.

Out of the pocket of his jacket, he pulled a small ring. "Callie Lee, you royal pain in my britches, will you make me the happiest man in all of Texas and become my wife?"

"You serious?"

"Dead serious. I want to marry you right this second."

"It's Sunday morning. Everyone is in church."

"Fine, then. We'll do it tomorrow. I wouldn't want to get in the way of souls getting saved."

"This is crazy."

"Yep."

"You're crazy."

"For you. Say yes and let me know you feel the same for me."

"I sure do."

He rose from his knees and dropped his mouth to hers, kissing her so hard she fell back on her elbows on the desk, and Jasper nearly fell on top of her. He scooped a hand around her waist and used the other to hold them up, leaned back on the sheriff's desk.

***

Callie

The whole length of him pressed against her as she lay back on the desk. Jasper's strong thighs pushed her legs apart, and she felt him grind against her. Like he'd blown on ashes, she felt that old familiar tingle start up again.

"Take me right now," she whispered in his ear.

Jasper groaned, his forehead pressed to hers. "I am trying to be a gentleman."

"I don't want to marry a gentleman. I want to marry you."

He took a great handful of her skirt and lifted it up over her legs. She watched his face go from nervous to overcome with desire. His eyes flared, and he chewed on his lip for a moment as more of her legs were revealed to him. Her stockings only went up to her thighs, leaving the rest of her flesh bare.

"Goddamn," he breathed. "You're more than a man can take."

"I disagree. And I think you should try."

"I will not make love to you until you're my wife," he said with great solemnity. "But that don't mean we can't do other things."

He ducked down and kissed the place where her stocking met her flesh, then turned his attention to the other thigh. The slightest bit of prickle grazed her skin from his jawline, but his lips were soft as he dragged them along her skin to the inside of her thigh and moved up.

She gasped as his fingers touched her womanhood.

"What if Luke comes in?" she managed.

"He'll probably give me a promotion," Jasper replied. "Don't worry about him. He's gone to church like he always does."

His hot breath warmed her skin, and she closed her eyes at the sensation. Jasper pushed, prodded, circled, explored, and wound her up like a music box with the way he used his hands and mouth on her. Her legs tensed, her back came up a bit off the table, and she reveled in him and the things he was doing to her. Under the willow that night, she'd been reminded that she was a woman—not just a mother, not a businesswoman, not a mayoral candidate, but a woman of flesh and blood and urges. He'd reminded her then, and reminded her again now.

If he'd moved to take her there and then, she'd have been delighted. If he'd been rough, she wouldn't have minded. Whatever Jasper wanted, he could have. But he didn't stray from his purpose. He stayed with her, focused on her, and didn't let up until Callie's pleasure ebbed, and she called out with her fingers wound in his red hair as it peaked.

"Jeepers," she breathed. He stood up and bent over her with a smile. "It's always the ones you don't expect."

He chuckled.

"I can return the favor," she whispered as she let her eyes move to his belt.

Jasper's hand clutched her waist tighter, but he shook his head. "Not now."

She lay on the desk, and noticed the messiness they'd made around them.

"Luke'll be mad we messed up his papers."

Jasper grabbed a handful of papers and threw them in the air. "Let him beat me to a pulp. I won't even feel it." He bent down and kissed the inside of her knee.

"Let me see that ring." She giggled.

He'd nearly forgotten, and fumbled to get it on her finger. The simple gold band had no adornments. She'd worn fancier jewels, but this one was the prettiest thing she'd ever seen. "I should get back to Nate."

"We both should, probably."

Callie smiled. "Let's go tell him you're gonna be his daddy, for real and forever."

Not much later, Jasper knelt on the floor of Nate's room and hugged the little boy hard. The kid most likely didn't truly realize what was happening, but when Callie had took his sweet little face in her hands and told him she was going to marry Jasper and they were going to go live in the house by the creek with the swing and Jasper was going to be his daddy, Nate hugged Jasper. Whatever he understood, it was enough.

And then they all sat together on the floor and played blocks. Callie looked at the ring on her finger and smiled, her heart swelling with happiness. This was a family, a fine one. They'd have a good life.

"I suppose I'll have to pack up these rooms." Callie looked around.

"You gonna miss it?"

"I'll still be here every day. I won't miss these rooms, though they hold lots of memories."

"Good ones?"

"Good and bad," she said. Then she laughed. "Remind me to tell you the story of how Haven went out the window in the hall closet one time."

"What?"

Callie shook her head. "Oh, this saloon. I do love it. But I think I will also love taking my coffee on a porch overlooking hills that lead down to a creek."

"And a boy on a swing."

"That too."

"I am truly sorry about Braxton. I know you and he had plans."

"We did," she said. Nate made a choo-choo sound and crashed his train into her leg. "But when all is said and done, I think this is the way it was supposed to be. The three of us."

"I think you're right."

He stayed there, in those rooms, with them all day, except for when he ran out to bring back some dinner. They talked and played and ate together, and it was the best time either could remember. He'd be a good father to the boy. Heck, he was already a good father, and the only one Nate had known.

Once they'd tucked Nate into his bed, Jasper kissed Callie. "I'll see myself out."

"You could stay. I mean, we're getting married tomorrow. What's one more day?"

"Stop tempting me." He grinned. "Good night."

"Good night."

"First thing in the morning, I'm going to tell the whole world."

"Me too."

CHAPTER TWENTY

Callie

Word of Braxton's death flowed fast through town, and there were a good number of pitying faces and consoling comments for Callie when she walked down the street to the clinic in the morning. Funny how the sadness about his death hadn't left her, but the sense of hopelessness had. Her heart wanted to explode with happiness over getting married to Jasper.

If it hadn't been for the strain in her friendship with Haven, Callie would have felt all right.

But oh, how she didn't want to face Haven.

To do so, she had to summon all her courage. Knowing she'd hurt her best friend so deeply felt horrible. Haven had been by her side like an iron statue from the very beginning of their relationship, and Callie hadn't repaid her well.

Callie went to the clinic first thing in the morning.

"Nurse Uppity," she called. "You in here?"

"Callie," Doc said, coming from upstairs. "Can I

help you?"

"Is Haven here?"

"In back. I was sorry to hear about Braxton."

"You and everyone else, but I appreciate the sentiment. I'd like to find a way to honor him. Say goodbye, somehow."

"Let me know if I can help at all. I liked that grumpy bastard."

"Me too." Haven walked out of the closet in the back of the clinic. When she saw Callie, her eyes turned angry.

"Come on in," Doc invited her. "Would you like some coffee?"

Callie looked past him. "If I come in, are you gonna stab me with one of your doctor scalpels?"

"Maybe," Haven answered.

Doc looked between the two women. "Do I need to be here?"

"Nope," the two women said in unison.

Doc lit out of the clinic like a man running for his life.

Callie held up her hands. "If you're gonna slice me, go ahead and do it."

"Don't tempt me," Haven said. "I nearly shot Hank, you know."

"I know."

"I might do the same to you, I'm so mad. Not only that you didn't tell me about Braxton, but really, what on earth were you were thinking?"

"I wanted to tell you about Jack."

"But you didn't." Haven was hurt; that was obvious. "We tell each other everything."

"You've been so sad since you lost the baby,"

Callie said. "I didn't want to make it worse."

Haven closed her eyes. "And the ridiculousness with Hank?"

"I was thinking about everyone except myself."

"From where I stood, it looked like you were having a fine time. I never thought I'd see that red dress again in my lifetime."

Callie blurted, "Jeepers, Haven. I thought if Hank and I said we were getting married, Jasper would leave me be, and you'd stop thinking whatever it is you still think about Hank."

"I don't think about Hank." The words came too fast, too defensively, for Callie to believe them.

"That is a bold-faced lie, Haven. He's the fork in the road you'll always wonder about—what would have happened if you'd chosen him over Matthew."

"I'd never have chosen him over Matthew."

"But you could have."

"What is wrong with having a thought to escape to sometimes?" Haven asked. "Life is hard on occasion. You should know that better than anyone. A daydream never hurt anyone."

"Except Matthew." Callie stepped close. "You're caught up in your own pain, I know, and that's understandable, but Matthew looks ready to throw himself off a cliff over it all. For God's sake, you were wearing that pin."

"And now it's gone somewhere in the dirt. Did you come here to lecture me about my husband?"

Haven wasn't going to budge, so Callie would. "I came here to tell you you'll soon be able to lecture me about mine."

Haven's eyes got wide.

"I'm going to marry Jasper. He talked me into it."

"Oh, Callie." Her mean expression melted, and her hands went to her mouth.

"And we're going to do it tonight. And it won't be right if you're not there standing by my side, even if we're spitting mad at each other while it happens."

"You know I'll be there."

"Good."

Haven sighed. "Do you have a dress?"

"I have the red one," Callie said with complete sincerity, but hoped it would make her friend laugh.

It worked. Haven actually laughed out loud. "I dare you to get married in that."

"I'd be struck by lightning if I stepped in a church in that."

"You could wear my white dress with the little flowers," Haven said.

"I don't think I need to wear white."

"But you do need something beautiful." Haven stepped up to Callie and embraced her. "You deserve it. You're a disaster, but you're my best friend and I'm so happy for you. And you need to tell me everything, every detail."

Callie looked to the door to make sure Doc was gone.

"There are a few details I shouldn't tell."

"Callie!" Haven squealed. "When? Oh, tell me later. Let's find you a dress!"

***

Jasper

"Gee whiz, Matthew, you look like you faced a bull and lost."

Matthew's face was bruised purple, and his lip was cut. He'd taken a lot of hits, but seeing him in the aftermath made Jasper realize just how many, and grateful it hadn't been worse. He was still alive, thank goodness. Injuries or not, he'd come to work. He sat outside the jail on the rocking chair, face tilted up to the sun and eyes closed.

"Feels like it too." Matthew winced a bit as he opened his eyes and shifted to see Jasper. "Doc says I got a cracked rib."

"Lucky Hank didn't kill you."

"Lucky I didn't kill him either. I wanted to."

"I know."

"I'm awful sorry I was rough to you," Matthew said. "Shoving and all."

"I forgive you." Jasper stepped directly in front of Matthew, so the battle-scarred man wouldn't have to turn his head for the next part of the reason he'd come. "In fact, what are your plans this evening?"

Matthew shrugged. "Probably sitting at home with Haven fussing over me."

"The two of you all right?"

Matthew actually smiled a bit. "We will be, I think. Once I force her to sit down and talk to me. All night long, if that's what it takes."

"How about, before that happens, you go get dressed in your Sunday best and be my best man?"

Matthew rocked forward and sat up, though

Jasper saw him wince again. "You serious?"

"As I've ever been."

"Hot damn," Matthew got to his feet carefully and gave Jasper a hug. "She actually said yes."

"She did."

"And you didn't have to beg."

"I begged a little." Jasper grew warm from head to toe at the memory of Callie laying before him in the jail. If that had been begging, he'd be happy to spend the rest of his life on his knees begging her.

"Ah," Matthew said.

"What?"

"You're blushing."

Jasper cleared his throat. "I am overcome with joy. Get your head out of the gutter, Frank."

"Good man."

The next few hours spun, and soon he was headed to the church. Callie walked next to him, looking like a flower in a yellow dress with lace trim.

"We're crazy," she said.

"Probably."

Outside the church, a small crowd had gathered. Luke, the Franks, Doc, the boys from the saloon, even Carolee and Jeb Gorman made an appearance.

Hank was nowhere to be found. Callie looked for him, Jasper saw it, but the scoundrel wasn't there.

Nate had been sitting on the steps, but came running toward Callie and Jasper, smiling and showing them a Y-shaped stick and a basket full of flower petals.

"I hear you'd like to get married." Reverend Crane came down the steps.

"If you'll have a couple of troublemakers like us," Jasper replied. He'd been slacking in getting himself to church every Sunday, but he meant to remedy that.

"These doors are open to all. Come on in."

It was hardly a formal ceremony, and happened quick. The reverend's wife played a nice piano piece while Luke urged Nate forward to throw some wildflower petals on the ground. Then Callie came down the aisle, with Doc giving her away to Jasper. Haven and Matthew flanked the couple, and the reverend wrapped things up without too much flowery phrasing.

It was simple, it was lively, and it was real.

"I pronounce you husband and wife," the reverend said. "Jasper, you finally get to kiss your bride." There was a twinkle in the reverend's eye, and Jasper caught his tease. "Make it a good one."

"I mean to."

Callie giggled. She handed her bouquet over to Haven, readying for the kiss.

Before God and everyone who mattered to them, he kissed her and sealed the promise of a lifetime.

CHAPTER TWENTY~ONE

Hank

A wagon adorned with flowers and ribbons waited outside the church when the newlyweds made their exit, husband and wife at last. Callie laughed at the sight, and Hill gave an elaborate bow from the seat before he jumped down to the ground, feigning a wobble in his knees.

"Ain't as young as I used to be," he exclaimed.

Nate rushed toward the wagon, but Haven caught him. "Oh no you don't. You're going to spend the night out at our place. And tomorrow you can ride Echo until your mama and papa come for you." She winked at them.

"Thank you," Jasper said.

"Happy to do it," Matthew said, poking Nate in the side and earning a giggle.

The Franks looked, for once, unified about something.

Callie and Jasper climbed into the wagon.

"Now don't you get lost," Hill called.

"It ain't even a quarter mile!" Jasper called back. "I can see it from here."

"Men get stupid with love," Luke said.

"You're all real funny." Jasper sat next to his bride and took the reins. "I hope you're as funny tomorrow."

There was a little more friendly banter, more cheering, and the newly married Tanners drove off down the road to town. The rest of the crowd dispersed. Haven held Nate's little hand and helped him up onto a horse to ride in front of Matthew.

Hank saw it all from where he hid, peering out from the shed behind the church. He saw the tight-knit group and their collective happiness, and was glad for it. They'd had enough hard times. Even Haven and Matthew seemed happy as they rode off with Nate holding the reins of Matthew's horse.

That he hadn't attended the wedding and been there in person to see Callie happily wed would always be a regret he carried, but he had more pressing issues. Maybe it was because he was the odd man out, but Hank was certain he was the only person around who had noticed the lone figure standing off a ways, watching the revels with quiet stillness.

He'd shadowed Ellie as soon as word of the impending wedding had started to make it's way through town. He'd been certain she was going to do something to stop it, but she hadn't. She'd carried on with her day, and then she'd walked over to the church.

Ellie didn't move until after the wagon pulled

away, and the rest of the friendly group dispersed. She watched with no expression on her face. What was she playing at? He'd stayed low all day, keeping his eyes on her. He'd thought for sure she was going to do something to interrupt the ceremony when she'd approached the church, but she'd simply positioned herself beneath some trees and not moved.

She'd watched, and he'd watched her until the wagon was out of sight and she headed back in the direction of town.

Good. Maybe she'd go home with him and perhaps remember that people took their places in life, and hers was with Charles.

His own place remained to be seen. He didn't seem to fit in Cricket Bend, even if a part of him thought it might be nice to. He'd never had a hard time fitting someplace before—he was slick enough to charm those who needed to be charmed to find himself a place in any city, and any city he didn't like he up and walked away from.

Cricket Bend was different. This town, this dusty little collection of people, he cared about.

He owed Callie Lee—now Calliope Rose Tanner—the world.

A feeling nagged him. Something he felt in his bones said not to trust Ellie Graham. He looked the way the wagon had gone, he could still see the dust it had kicked up. Jasper and Callie had gone back to the saloon for the night, and tomorrow they'd begin their lives together, making their way and their place in the world as one.

He walked toward the saloon. He'd keep an eye

on things for the night.

It was the least he could do. All he'd done since he got to town was complicate things.

After Callie and Jasper went into the saloon, and Hill came to take the horses from the wagon over to the livery for the night, Hank walked the perimeter of the building. The whole town was quiet, the night was warm, and things were fine.

The crickets were singing, loud and happy.

The saloon had been his at one time. As such, he was familiar with its layout, and aware that out back there was a bench made of several crates that had been nailed together. Men used it to take air sometimes, or to talk of things they couldn't risk others overhearing. Hank went there, and sat down. It would be a long night, sitting and watching. But he would do it.

Nothing bad would happen that night.

He sat for a long while, listening to the crickets and waiting to hear anything out of place.

He got up to answer the call of nature, and stepped into the shadows cast by the restaurant.

He smirked a bit when he thought of Callie and Jasper upstairs. A wedding night like they were sure to have would be explosive. He wondered if Jasper realized how lucky he truly was to have a woman who understood the art of pleasure the way Callie did. Likely, Jasper already did. If not, the man was in for the kind of surprise that could keep a smile on a man's face for days at a time.

He tucked himself away, and turned back in the direction of his watch point.

Something moved in the dark. His head hurt.

Things went black.

CHAPTER TWENTY-TWO

Callie

As Jasper drove the decorated wagon up in front of the saloon, Callie looked at her building. After this night, she would move to a new home—a real home. The last time she'd lived somewhere other than above a saloon or in a hotel room had been over fifteen years ago when she'd left the only home she'd ever known. Jasper's house, the house he'd told her he had built with a long-off dream of her becoming his wife, was warm and fine. It would be a wonderful home for Nate to grow up in, and if they had more children together it would be a house fit to raise a family in and around.

For one last night, though, she would sleep in the saloon.

Hill would come by for the horses later, he'd said, so Jasper wouldn't have to deal with them on his wedding night. In the meantime, Jasper tied the horses outside the saloon so they wouldn't wander off, and followed Callie inside the swinging doors of the saloon. Once they were inside, Callie closed the doors and slid the wooden board in place to shut them for the night. Saloons rarely closed, but she'd had an occasion or two to have to close up before.

Tonight counted as an occasion worthy of closing Callie's.

Ben had left a few of the lamps lit for them. He'd also left a bottle and two glasses on the bar, which had been polished to shine.

"Would you like a drink, Mr. Tanner?"

"I would, Mrs. Tanner." Jasper's smile couldn't have been missed from ten miles away. He stepped quickly to his bride and pulled her close, kissing her sweetly. "I think we should have a drink to new beginnings."

"In that case, I'll get the good stuff." Callie wiggled from his arms and went behind the bar, ducking down to pull out one specific bottle of brown liquor. "Barrel-aged whiskey from Kentucky. I keep it on hand for Doc, but he won't mind sharing just this once."

"Kind of him."

"He's a kind man."

They drank, not saying anything.

"What will your Ma say when she hears you up and got yourself married?"

"She'll be delighted. She likes children. Nate's already got a passel of cousins."

Cousins. Nate would have cousins and a grandmother. If she had any lingering doubts about becoming a wife, knowing that Nate would have a real family erased them.

Jasper finished his drink, and licked a bit of the whiskey off his lip.

Every part of her body wanted him. Callie came around the bar, took his hand, and led him upstairs to her small room. It was dark, so she lit a candle, then opened the window to let in the light from the last of the sunset.

"Mrs. Tanner, may I say you look beautiful tonight?"

Callie grinned. "Mrs. Tanner. I like the sound of that."

"Me too."

"I'm jumpy as a frog," she whispered, but he had gone over to stand by the bed and didn't hear her. The man in the room with her—sitting down on the bed not six feet behind her as she watched—was her husband. Jasper was her husband, for better or for worse. The idea of him being there, so close and about to touch her again, made her whole body come awake.

Damn the past. They would start new, and start that night.

Callie unhooked the dress she wore, dropped it to the floor, and let her underthings follow.

With the feel of air on bare skin, she got tingles all over.

She turned to face her husband. He sat on the edge of the bed, staring at her. His eyes got even bigger as he took in her body. Callie chuckled and put her hands on her hips. "Ain't like you've never seen me before," she said.

"Just realizing that I've never seen you without your clothes on," he said.

"Oh!" Then she realized. "I never took them off completely," she answered with a shrug. "Usually there wasn't time." She turned her back to him, looked flirty over her shoulder, and shook her bottom a bit. "You like what you see?"

He stood up, shirt unbuttoned and untucked. "Don't do that."

"Do what?"

"Put on an act. You don't have to with me. You're the most beautiful thing I ever seen."

She took a few steps toward him and rested a hand on his lower stomach. "Don't you go gettin' all soft on me."

"I don't think you have to worry about that," he said, taking her hand and moving it lower to the front of his pants.

"Oh my," she answered. "I guess not."

He smiled.

"And, for what it's worth, Mr. Tanner, like I said before, you ain't so bad yourself."

She slid his shirt off him, revealing his strong chest and arms. His skin, lightly freckled in places, was smooth and warm under her fingers as she touched his chest.

"Are you nervous?" he asked. "You can tell me if you're nervous. 'Cause I'm nervous. I'm real damn nervous. I'd be shakin' in my boots if I was still wearing them."

"I'll pay you, if it makes you more comfortable," Callie teased.

A loud laugh burst from him, and the sound of it made Callie laugh as well.

Jasper's warm hands came up and took hold of

her shoulders, clutching her. He dropped his face to hers. "This one's on the house," Jasper replied, and then took her mouth with his.

When they'd been together under the willow, she'd been in charge. In her past career, she'd always been the one in charge. It was the role of the working girl, to get the men in the room, give them what they wanted, and send them out the door happy customers in as quick a time as possible. This time, in this room this night, it was immediately clear that Jasper was going to be in charge, and Callie relished it. The way he kissed her, deep and long, pulling at pieces of her she'd forgotten existed, made her knees wobble a bit. At last, she had the trust and freedom to let him take control.

He moved them both, kissing all the way, to the bed and sat down on the edge, pulling her to him and locking her tight while he kissed her neck and the skin between her breasts. Callie's head rolled back at the sensations. His hands slid around her hips and over her bottom, roaming lightly.

"You better not ever stop kissing on me," she whispered.

"Ain't planning on it," he replied, with his lips against her breast. "I'll never get enough of the taste of you."

He pulled her down with him, rolled over her, and held her by the hands against the mattress.

His mouth found her neck, and he kissed behind her ear.

For the ferocity of his lovemaking, there was also such sweetness. Perhaps she'd never known what it was to be with a lover who valued her as a whole being, not just a body for pleasure. Every place his hands touched, every spot his lips kissed, felt anointed and blessed. This man, who was paying such extra close attention to her every need, who breathed when she breathed, was of all things her husband.

She shifted her body and opened herself to him.

Heavens. She was nervous. As nervous as if they'd never done this before, which they had—many times.

Jasper kissed her, and held her lip in his as he joined his body with hers. Callie moaned into his mouth as he filled her. No matter how close he got to her, it would never again be enough. He moved slowly, gently, careful of her without being timid. That he knew what he was doing was a relief.

"I'm yours," she whispered.

"And I'm yours," he answered.

And then they lost their minds together.

There was no reason to hold anything back anymore.

Knowing no one was downstairs in the saloon, Callie called out as loud as she wanted with pleasure, and enjoyed every inch of him. Jasper claimed her, held her tight but relinquished control when she wanted it, and they owned each other for hours. They rolled around together, passion peaking, until the blankets fell off the bed and their two naked bodies lay sideways on the mattress.

He shivered, then lay still surrounded by the soft floral scent of the skin on her neck as his breathing returned to normal. He laid one hand on her stomach.

Callie glanced down at his fingers, stroking her lightly. "If we had a baby, you think it'd have blonde or red hair?"

"I want you to have lots of my babies," he whispered. "With hair of all colors."

"I'd like that too," she answered. "We could give Nate a whole passel of siblings to play with."

"That's a goal I don't mind working toward one bit."

"I didn't figure you'd have a problem with it."

A soft kiss, a satisfied exhale, and Jasper rested his head on the pillow next to her.

A little while later, they did it all over again.

And then one more time before falling into a hard sleep, wound together in the sheets. Curled against him, his chest against her back and his hand rested on the curve of her hip, Callie felt the happiest she'd ever been. They were going to have a good life together, and Nate would be the most loved child in all of Texas, if not the whole country.

CHAPTER TWENTY-THREE

Jasper

The heat woke him, and the odd feeling of wetness.

Before he even sat up, he wiped his damp brow.

He recognized it, then. It was sweat, pouring from him.

Oh God, the heat. It seared and it pushed and pulled, and seemed to suck all the moisture out of the air in one moment. Jasper leapt from the bed, only to start choking on the smoke that filled the room with a haze. His eyes tried to focus, but failed.

His new bride lay naked on the bed, sleeping on her belly sideways across the mattress. There was no time to revel in her beauty and what a lucky man he was. All he wanted to do was keep her safe.

"Callie." He threw on his discarded pants as he shook her and she shot up on the bed.

They'd thrown the blankets from the bed in their passion, and he nearly tripped over the pile as he dove for the door that connected Callie's room to Nate's. Still waking, he flung open the door and saw the small empty bed before he realized the boy wasn't there. He wasn't in the fire. Nate was safe with the Franks, blessedly far from this.

"What's wrong—happening—oh no."

Callie grabbed a dressing gown off the back of her door. It barely covered her, but there wasn't time to care about modesty.

Jasper went around her and grabbed the doorknob, then yelped and pulled back his hand. The knob felt hot enough to melt. He picked up the blanket on the ground and wrapped it around the knob to open the door.

Smoke pushed into the bedroom, coming in fast from the hall. Through it, Jasper saw the fire between them and the stairs. They were trapped, and the fire was raging.

"This way." Callie grabbed his arm, and pushed him into the hall the other direction. The hallway ended in a wall, but she waved away smoke as she went for another door and pushed it open. It was a small closet, hardly big enough for two people, but it had a small square window on the wall.

"We're going out this way," she said.

It seemed a crazy notion, but Callie charged ahead and reached up to open it. "There's an awning outside. It can hold us while we climb down."

"You sure?"

"No. I think so. It held Haven once."

"What?"

"Long story. Give me a boost."

Obeying his wife, Jasper hooked his hands and took her bare foot to boost her up. Head-first, Callie went out the window, and a moment later she peeked back in. "It'll hold." He reached up and grabbed the window frame, pulling himself up. Callie's hands grabbed him and pulled as well, and he just made it through the tight squeeze of the window.

"Help!" Callie hollered into the night as she stood up on the awning.

From there, they could see all of Cricket Bend and the land that stretched in miles all around it, looming like darkness until the point where it reached the bluer night sky.

Callie let a loud whistle, and he joined her in hollering.

Bodies came into the street below as the fire began to wake the citizens who lived in town. Down in the street, Jasper saw a few men who took rooms at the boarding house step out and look up with aghast faces. "Up here!"

"I'll get a ladder," Paul Archer yelled up, then ran off.

The outside wall of the saloon by the awning started to blacken. The fire would come through soon. They needed to get clear, and they didn't have time to wait for a ladder.

"I'm going to jump," Jasper said. "And then you'll jump and I'll catch you."

"I ain't afraid to break a leg," she said.

Smoke started to pour from the window.

Callie got down on her bottom and slid over the side of the awning. Jasper followed suit, and the two of them slipped over the side and fell to the ground with ungraceful thuds.

"Callie!"

Doc came running from his place, pulling up his suspenders even as he approached. He helped them both to their feet. "You all right?" he asked, looking closely at both of them and the place from where they'd fallen.

Callie coughed and nodded. "It's the whole upstairs."

"Anyone but you two in there? Ben or anyone?"

"Not tonight, thank god."

Flames burst out the windows in another moment and sent glass flying out over the street. Jasper grabbed Callie, holding her tight to him to block her with his back to the spray. He felt sharp pokes of pain, but fortunately they were just past where the majority of the glass fell.

Callie buried her face in his chest. He felt her ragged breathing. "Nate."

"He's as safe as can be. He's far from here with Haven, remember?"

"All his things. All my things. I'll have nothing left."

"Hush," Jasper said. Smoothing her hair, he kissed the top of her head. "It's just things. Things can be replaced." He put a hand on her cheek and looked into her eyes. "It's just things."

"What happened?"

Luke walked up, with mussed hair and bleary eyes. He'd taken the night shift, and the explosion must have woken him.

"That happened." Jasper indicated the saloon,

which was a solid wall of flame.

"You two all right?" They nodded. Luke touched their shoulders in relief. "Got any idea what started it?"

"We were sleeping," Jasper said. "Woke up from the heat and went out the window."

"It's spreading!" Paul Archer hollered down the street to Luke.

"The restaurant. The hardware store." Callie seemed to come back to life at the realization of the damage the flames could do to the rest of the town.

"Can we contain it?" Doc asked.

"We're gonna have to try," Luke said.

"Stay here," Jasper said to Callie.

"Like hell I will." She put her hands on her hips. "That is my saloon burning down and those are my neighbors and friends who run the businesses next door. I'm helping. Don't argue with me."

"Don't argue with her," Doc suggested.

"I will not argue with you," Jasper said.

"That's the secret to a happy marriage," Luke said.

"But you ain't dressed to fight a fire."

"Neither are you."

Neither of them wore much. Neither wore shoes of any kind, but Callie stood shivering wearing no more than a practically indecent slip of silk.

Luke handed his duster to Jasper. "Come on."

Doc pushed Callie toward the clinic. "Grab something from my things."

Before she split from them, Jasper kissed her. He hated to leave her side, but the town needed every set of hands it could get. He pulled on the jacket, wincing as it touched the small places where the fire had cut the bare skin on his back.

By the time Luke had wrangled enough people and dispatched Doc to take Hill's wagon and use it to haul barrels of water from the creek to be put on the fire, the flames had overcome the restaurant and caught on the hardware store walls.

"Forget the restaurant," Luke ordered. "I hate to do it, but we'll do best to get as much as we can out of the hardware store before it gets too bad."

A group of men rushed into the store, and started bringing items out and stacking them in the street. Tom Harmon didn't live in town. The poor man likely had no idea his business was going up in smoke.

"You all," Luke ordered. "Get water and, whatever you do, keep the fire from taking the bathhouse."

At last, there was some hope. The bathhouse stood about twenty feet from the wall of the restaurant. As the fire swept, Paul Archer and a handful of other men parked themselves there and watered every lick of flame that threatened to cross the line. Jasper joined them, hauling water toward the divide as fast as he could until his arms ached.

Reg and Virginia Spindler arrived to town. The owners of the bathhouse looked so afraid. Seeing them made the men work faster, haul more water, just to try and salvage something. The men with the buckets of water did all they could for as long as they could, but at least one wall of the building was going to burn.

"Get anything out that you can," Luke said to the

Spindlers. "And you might want to start praying."

The Spindlers rushed off, and Luke stopped for a moment.

"Sheriff," Jasper said. "You need to take a break?"

"I'm fine," Luke said. "Watching your town burn makes a man realize what things are really important."

"I hear you."

"Keep working on the bathhouse," he ordered. "But there's no stopping it from taking the hardware store. I'll find someone to ride out to Harmon's and let him know, and out to Matthew as well. The other Archers too."

Men rode out in all directions. With the energy of young men, Hill and Doc took off on horses that weren't even theirs to let folks know.

**

Callie

"Sweet Father—"

"What the hell happened to you?"

Jasper turned and saw Hank approaching them. He was stumbling, and holding his head. There was blood smeared on his forehead, and his shirt was torn open.

Hank groaned. "What happened?"

Callie threw up her hands. "Everything happened, Hank. It's all burning to the ground."

Among Doc's clothes, she'd found a pair of pants and a shirt that were both far too big but she'd tied them and it was good enough. Her feet were still bare, as all his shoes had also been too big. Cuts on her feet were the least of her worries.

The town was burning, fast.

Matthew and Haven arrived on horseback within a half-hour, trailing behind Hill. Nate rode on the front of Matthew's saddle with sleepy eyes that grew big and scared at the fire. Callie rushed for him and took him in her arms to hold him tight, the heavy weight of his growing body almost too much, except that in that moment he could have weighed a hundred pounds and she'd have held him forever. Haven stepped up behind Callie and put her arms around her friend and scooted them away from the direction the flames were heading.

Matthew headed for Jasper. "Where's Luke?"

"Gone into the boarding house and the other businesses," Jasper answered. "Making sure everyone is accounted for."

"There was no one in the saloon besides us," Callie said. "I'd closed up. Ben stays at the boarding house. Tom Harmon doesn't live in town. The Spindlers are over there."

"Where's Delia?" Jasper asked.

The mention of the widow made them all stop. All of them looked toward the fire. The restaurant was the middle of the three businesses, but it had been burning for a while.

"She lives in her upstairs rooms," Callie realized. "Moved in there after her husband died and she sold their house—oh no."

Jasper charged forward to the restaurant. Matthew jumped in front of him and stopped him.

"Not tonight you don't. See to your wife and son."

"Matthew!"

"I owe you one."

"For what?"

"For not arresting me for being drunk and disorderly."

The deputy took off at a run toward the restaurant. Jasper nearly followed him, but Callie caught his arm. She couldn't let him go after Matthew, couldn't risk never seeing him again.

"Doc's comin!" someone called. Doc rode fast leading the three Archer boys into town, and Jasper felt a bit of hope in his chest. More men could help. More water on the fire, more eyes looking for people who needed help. Every man or woman they could get could help.

Luke came out from the boarding house, leading a crowd of more people behind him. "What the hell is Matthew doing?"

"It's Delia," Callie said. "No one's seen her. We think she's still in there."

Luke's face lost all its color. He took a couple steps forward, just in time to see Matthew kick open the door to the restaurant and go inside.

Haven came running forward to the group just then. "Where is he—"

Luke grabbed her by the arm.

"I'm going with him." Jasper rushed forward.

There were not five seconds between the moment Matthew went in and when the building collapsed in on itself. Jasper had just about made it to the door, and jumped backward out of the way as the boards of fire crumbled, cracked, and seemed to melt as the two-story building lurched and half-sunk, a pile of burning boards.

Callie turned for Nate, who had been watching the fire with big eyes. As the building fell, Luke scooped him up in his arms.

Haven screamed at the sight of the collapse. The sound was terrible, like that of a person being tortured or murdered.

Jasper didn't move for a moment. Callie froze, terrified of the worst. She ran forward, sliding across the dirt to where he lay. He groaned.

"Son of a bitch, that hurt," he said as he pulled himself up.

Callie smacked him in the shoulder. "Don't you ever do something foolish like that again."

"Matthew." Jasper looked past her to the fire. "He's in there."

"I know," Callie said.

"Haven!"

Both of them turned at the sound of Luke calling his daughter's name. With Nate in his arms, he couldn't stop her fast enough. Haven charged forward past Callie toward the flames, pale as a ghost. Jasper tried to get up to stop her, but couldn't. From where she knelt, Callie reached for her, but missed.

Haven was heading into the fire—fearless, careless.

It was Hank who stopped her. With two arms locked around her waist, he lifted her off her feet and moved her back away from the fire to the group. She didn't make it easy on him, fighting and kicking and cursing his name. For a small woman, she struggled mightily, and even landed a few blows. Hank being Hank, he never let go.

"Please," Callie heard her beg. Her heart broke at Haven's sorrow.

"No," Hank said. "You're not dying too. Pipe down."

Jasper started to his feet. "I'm going in after him."

"No, you're not."

Hank lugged Haven, now limp and beaten, over to Callie and plopped her down in the dirt next to them like she weighed nothing. Weakened, Haven didn't argue. It was obvious she was already expecting the worst. Callie reached for her and Haven dropped her head into Callie's lap.

"God damn son of a bitch hellfire," Hank muttered.

"What are you going to do?" Jasper asked.

"I'm going into the goddamn fire," Hank hollered. Then he took a deep breath and did as he said he would: he walked directly to where the door of the restaurant still half-stood.

"That stupid man," Callie breathed.

"I should go with him."

"No," Callie begged.

"Matthew is the best friend I got in this world."

"And if you go in there and get killed tonight, I'll never speak to you again. Hank has gone in there, and if he can get Matthew out he will."

"You sure about that?"

Callie put a hand on Haven's back. "Actually, I am."

CHAPTER TWENTY-FOUR

Hank

Someday, Hank would stop walking willingly into fires.

"Damn. Damn, damn, damn."

What remained of the restaurant was no more than an inferno, and it was a shame. Delia Lance was an attractive woman who made a damn fine meat pie and greeted everyone like they were family no matter how busy she was or who they were. The woman deserved better than this. So did Harmon's Hardware and Callie's. Poor Callie. The saloon was all but gone.

Somewhere in the rumble lay Matthew, probably hurt if not already dead.

His anger threatened to erupt, and his head throbbed.

First, he needed to find Matthew and get him out if he could.

Then, he'd go track down the person he felt sure

was responsible for starting the fire in the first place. He'd heard the swish of skirts before feeling the thump that had knocked him out in the dirt. He had a pretty good idea who would have reason to do something of this nature.

Hank had spent enough time around terrible people in his life.

Sweating and swearing, Hank stepped over furniture—what had been tables and chairs, the ones closest to the door, he assumed. The staircase that led up to the second floor, where Delia had lived since the death of her husband, had fallen, and part of the second floor fell with it. If Matthew was trapped, he was beneath that.

Flames licked higher than his head and the scorching heat would have driven anyone else out. A burning flicker scraped his arm, and he pulled it toward himself.

By morning, the boarding house and saloon would be nothing but ash.

Something, a few boards, moved near where the stairs had collapsed.

Matthew had made it in, and had been at least to the staircase when it collapsed. Now he lay on the ground, pinned and dazed. Hank saw the man try and get up, but then he fell back down. He coughed and struggled, and a burning board was only inches from his legs. He was already hurt from their fight, and the expression of agony on his face made Hank feel bad for beating the tar out of him.

The heat was horrible. Hank's instincts said to flee as fast as he go. He could do it—bail out, stumble onto the street and say he'd not seen

Matthew and it had been too terrible inside. He could leave the man to burn and, in the aftermath, pick up the pieces of Haven's shattered life as well as his own.

He was not proud of himself for the thought.

When she'd fought him, desperate to get into the fire to Matthew, he'd seen her eyes. Damn, but that look would haunt him for the rest of his life if he didn't do the right thing. Cursed Haven, always making him want to be better.

She'd been so nearly in his grasp that night.

She'd promised him she'd be his, if he'd just help her save Matthew and her father from Philip Frank. Hank had done it, switched the script and Philip had died in the dirt in front of a burning barn. And he'd seen Haven's eyes, seen her pain and resignation, and he'd slipped away into the smoke and ridden off. He'd ridden hard, all the way to New Orleans, where the whiskey and card games were constant and the noise of the city could distract him from most any sad or fearful thoughts he had.

Except thoughts of Haven. Those never left.

Matthew groaned.

Hank needed to be the man Haven thought he could be, and the man Callie thought he was.

He jumped forward and kicked the beam aside, giving Matthew room to stand.

"Get up," Hank ordered.

He offered Matthew his hand. Matthew hesitated.

"Why you helpin' me?"

"Don't argue with me. Just get up."

"You're doing this for her."

"I'd do anything for her, even if that includes keeping you alive." Matthew took Hank's hand and let him pull him up. Hank bent down and let Matthew loop an arm over his shoulder. "Watch where you step. This place isn't gonna last long."

"Delia…" Matthew choked out the word before coughing again.

"Is she here?"

"Her room is up there." Matthew pointed to the second floor. Without the stairs, getting to the second floor would be tricky. The building wasn't going to last long.

"Can you walk?" Hank asked. When Matthew nodded, he let him stand on his own. "Grab that table."

Matthew looked pained, but did as Hank said. Hank brought over another one and the two men stacked it on top of the first. "Not a far jump to the railing from there."

Hank started to climb up, but Matthew stopped him. "I'll do it."

"You got a busted rib and look like hell."

"I look worse than I feel."

"I doubt it."

"Porter!" Matthew cried. "Get the hell out of my way."

"Fine."

"And be ready to catch."

Matthew climbed up on the two tables, braced himself, and jumped over to the remaining part of the second floor. Landing, he looked down to Hank, and then vanished into a hallway.

Hank stood in the fire, waiting and praying for Matthew to return. The back wall of the restaurant cracked, ready to fall.

"Got her!"

Matthew carried Delia's prone body, just barely. She didn't move, but hung in his arms like a rag doll. Matthew bit at his lip against the weight and the pain of his own broken body, but didn't stop moving. He knelt down. "You're gonna have to catch her."

Hank held out his arms. "Drop her."

Matthew slid Delia over the edge as gently as he could, but she still fell heavy into Hank's arms, nearly taking him to the ground.

Glass shattered.

Wood cracked.

"Matthew," Hank called. "Get down here now."

Matthew still held a hand to his ribs, but crouched down and jumped down to the floor, ignoring the stacked tables altogether.

"Go," Hank ordered.

It wasn't far to the front door. Around them, the walls fell. Hank used Delia to push Matthew forward toward the one spot of outside he could still see, the place where the door had been left open. Out there, he saw the street and people running and a wagon. It was so close, he could practically hear the crickets.

CHAPTER TWENTY~FIVE

Callie

The last pieces of the saloon fell, and there was no holding back the tears that fell onto her cheeks. It was just a building, she reminded herself. It could be rebuilt.

The reminder didn't stop the heartache.

The remainder of the restaurant and hardware store would follow suit. Any minute now they'd crack and fall in on themselves, burning to no more than embers.

And people she cared about were still inside.

Callie waited for Hank and Matthew to come out of the danger. She wasn't alone. Most everyone who had seen them go in waited to see if they'd come out again. Jasper had sat up and gone toward the fire, promising he wouldn't go inside. He wanted to. She saw it in the way he paced, tense as a wound spring. He looked back at her and Nate, reminding himself of good reasons not to go in after his best friend. Without them there, she knew he'd have gone right into the fire. He'd have run toward death to save his friend.

Callie clutched Haven close to her, smoothing the younger woman's hair. No tears came from Haven. All she could do was shake with fear.

Luke stood right behind them. Nate sat in his arms, his head resting on the tall man's shoulder.

There was nothing any of them could do but wait.

The powerlessness felt terrible. Callie whispered down to Haven, "It'll be all right, sugar."

Haven shook her head. "I don't think so. Shouldn't they be out by now? What's taking so long?"

"If they come out, they might need you. They might be hurt."

Haven seemed to hear the words, and swallowed. "Yes. I know."

"Look," Luke said, bending down and setting Nate on the ground by Callie.

Ash-covered and coughing, Matthew stumbled out of the restaurant remains. He nearly fell as he jumped down the stairs, but stayed on his feet. Just two steps behind Matthew, Hank carried a woman out of the fire.

Haven stood up, mouth wide open. She took off running toward them. The minute Haven reached her husband, they fell into each other's arms. He was weak and they fell to their knees together with Haven supporting most of his weight as she sobbed into his shoulder, but he was alive.

A tear skimmed down Callie's cheek.

There was always hope.

In the middle of a fire that destroyed a quarter of a town, something had shifted and the Franks were together again, embracing on their knees in the street. Love couldn't be stopped by danger or death, not when it was real.

Jasper was running too. When he reached them, he took Delia from Hank, letting the man bend over and breathe. Doc was already on the move, tending to the prone woman.

"It's Delia," Luke called out. "They got her."

Doc took Delia away from the fire into the clinic. Haven and Matthew followed.

Jasper went to a barrel and cupped his hand into the water for a drink. Callie realized her own thirst, and that Nate was probably thirsty too. The heat in the air surrounded them, and the smoke poked at her lungs.

How she loved him.

Carrying Nate in her arms, Callie walked over to her husband. She didn't say anything, just wrapped her arms around him.

"What was that for?"

"For loving me. And for being here right now, alive."

"Shoot," he said. "I been alive and loving you for a long time and didn't get kissed for it."

"Get ready for the rest of your life."

"I can't wait. Little bug, take a drink of water."

The buildings finally collapsed, sending smoke and dust into the air. Callie ducked down and pulled Nate to her, and Jasper stood over the two of them to shield as best he could.

When the smoke cleared, burning wood remained.

Nate cried from fear and exhaustion. His wails were the only sound Callie could hear. No one else moved. No one said a word. She picked the boy up and swayed back and forth, whispering a song to him.

Luke called out to the gathered people. "I need a couple volunteers to keep watch with me, but everyone else, go on home. We'll handle the damage in the morning. There's no more we can do tonight."

Callie's eyes started to close. Nate was falling asleep as she rocked him, his cries now only whimpers. His head hung at an uncomfortable looking angle, his little lips in a pout. Jasper put an arm around her. The ride to his place would take a bit, and all three of them were too tired.

"You all go on home too," Luke said.

"It's too far a ride," Jasper said, indicating Nate.

"Whyn't you sleep in the jail for a spell? I know it probably ain't the wedding night you hoped for, but there's two cots."

"I'd sleep right here in the dirt right now," Callie said. "A cot sounds like heaven."

When Nate was tucked into one of the jail cots, and Callie sat beside him and yawned, Hank showed up at the jail. Haven and Matthew were right behind him.

"Sheriff," he said.

Luke thrust out a hand to him. Hank looked unsure of the gesture.

"I want to say thank you, Porter. Going in after

Matthew was a stupid thing to do, but I don't know if he or Delia would be alive if you hadn't."

"Don't mention it," Hank said. "That's not why I'm here. I have information."

"What kind of information?" Jasper stood up from where he'd been kneeling to kiss Nate's forehead.

Callie saw something on the scoundrel's face. "Say what you came to say, Hank."

He shook his head. "Why don't you get some sleep, Callie?"

Jasper stood up and put a hand on her shoulder. "You and Nate get some sleep now. You don't need to worry about anything else."

"Don't worry?" Callie felt like she'd explode. The only thing keeping her from screaming was the fear of waking Nate. "My saloon just burned. Other than you and Nate, I don't have much left. So whatever you have to say, Hank, I am absolutely dying to hear it."

Resigned, Hank looked at Luke. "I know who did this."

"What do you mean?"

"Someone started this fire, Sheriff."

No one had thought of that. There hadn't been time to ponder why the fire happened, only to scramble and survive it.

"Why would anyone do that?" Haven asked.

"To get to you." Hank looked right at Callie.

Callie froze. "Who?"

"Someone who's hurt, and jealous, and mean. Someone who smells like lilies and wears boots with heels just like the ones Haven wears."

233

"You noticed the boots."

"Not the boots. The sound they make. I know that sound."

Of all the people in all the world, Callie would never have thought it possible that what Hank was about to say could ever be true. She realized the man who held her hand was the great love of Ellie's life, and Callie her sworn enemy.

"Ellie told me I better leave you be," Callie whispered to Jasper.

Jasper huffed.

"You're accusing Ellie." Luke looked to Hank. "You think Ellie Graham did this?"

"I know she did," Hank said. "She wanted Jasper, and she hates Callie."

"I'm going to need more than that." Luke's brow furrowed.

"She told me if I didn't drop out of running for mayor, and let Jasper be, she'd release a list of my former clients in the newspaper," Callie announced.

"That's why you dropped out?" Matthew asked.

"Hank is right, Luke. She's got it in her to do something like this."

"Who hit you?" Jasper asked.

Hank looked at him. He'd wiped away the blood on his head long ago.

"Someone in skirts, and boots with heels. I was out back of the saloon. My plan was to keep an eye on things for the night, and then—I was on the ground."

"Ellie."

"Ellie. She wanted to see you hurt. You don't even know how badly."

"She nearly got her wish."

CHAPTER
TWENTY~SIX

Jasper

"Goddammit."

Jasper stepped away from Callie, shaking his head even as the haunting realization that the accusation was correct struck him. Ellie had been upset when he'd left her in the barn, and had been acting strangely for weeks. He'd known her his whole life, and she—more than perhaps anyone else he'd ever known—could absolutely do something as horrific as start a fire and put people in danger.

"This is my fault," he said. Pushing himself away from Callie, he started to walk back and forth across the jail. "Ellie did this."

"You don't know," Luke said. "I'm going to need some proof before—"

"Luke, Ellie did this. I know she did. And she did it for me."

"Now hold on a second." Matthew spoke up. "Ellie did this for Ellie. She's been meaner than a rattler since we were kids. You just never noticed 'cause she let you get up her skirt."

If Luke hadn't been standing there, Jasper wouldn't have even been embarrassed by the statement. Just about everyone in town knew of their past relationship.

"I was dumb." Jasper shrugged.

Matthew nodded. "Boys are always dumb. Men don't get much smarter."

Hank chuckled. Matthew turned to him. "You of all people know I'm right."

"Oh, you're right," Hank answered. "It's amazing most of us make it through the day."

Matthew looked at Hank. "I still don't like you."

"I didn't expect you did."

Matthew turned back to Jasper. "Where's Ellie now?"

"I would have said at home, but I doubt she went back there."

"Where else would she go?"

Pages and pages of memories ran through his mind. Of all the places they'd ever gone, the one Ellie had liked best had always been the willow. There, she'd always seemed more at ease than anywhere else.

Jasper gulped. "I know where we can find her. We gotta go now."

"I'll go with you," Matthew said as he tried to stand up. Haven put her hands on his shoulders and stopped him.

"So will I," Luke said.

Jasper looked at his two fellow lawmen. Both their hearts were as big as oceans, but this last battle he needed to fight without either of them. "No. You two take care of the rest of the town. Everyone else here, they need you."

"You're not going alone," Callie said.

"Nope," Jasper said. "Hank's coming with me. If he agrees."

"The woman hit me with a board," Hank said. "Damn right I'm coming with you."

Jasper kissed Callie quickly. "I will be back soon. She won't hurt me."

He and Hank rode out.

Where the creek snaked north for a few hundred yards, the astonishing willow tree came into sight, hanging over the bend in the creek. The young people of Cricket Bend had been known to sneak away to its secrecy under cover of night, and Jasper remembered the careless nights as he rode up, with Hank next to him.

"Hold back," Jasper said to him. "Maybe I can talk to her."

"And if you can't?"

"I trust you'll come up with something."

Hank tied his horse and went around the weeds. Jasper tied Dorothy and approached until he came under the vines of the tree.

Ellie sat in the dirt, her back against the tree's trunk. Her knees were up to her chest, and she hugged them. The staunch pain in the ass was all gone, replaced by nothing more than a wounded little girl.

"Ellie," Jasper called.

She closed her eyes and leaned her head back against the bark at the sound of his voice. She made no effort to flee, or to argue.

He went closer to her, moving slow.

Ellie was different, not bothering to posture or holler. The fight seemed to have gone out of her altogether.

"Are you all right?" he asked.

"I should ask you the same question."

"I'm fine, considering someone tried to kill me tonight."

"It wasn't you," she said. "I bet you've come to arrest me."

"What on Earth would make you do something so stupid and dangerous? You could have killed someone."

"That's the funny part," she said. "I wanted to. I wanted her dead and I lit that bottle and threw it and then—as soon as it landed and the fire started, I knew it had been a mistake. But it was too late, and I ran. Is anyone hurt?"

"The saloon, restaurant, and hardware store are gone. The bathhouse is a wreck. Delia Lance nearly burned to death. Matthew too."

Ellie closed her eyes. "I didn't mean for all that to happen."

"Well, it did. You could have taken down the whole town. What the hell were you thinking?"

He expected rage, tears, something.

The answer she gave was one he didn't expect.

"We were happy once."

"We were kids."

"But we were happy. I was happy with you."

"People grow up," he said. "People change."

"Mama used to tell me I could have anything

money could buy."

"Money ain't happiness."

"And it couldn't buy me you."

"I'm sorry things went the way they went," Jasper said. "I swear I am, Ellie."

With what appeared to be great effort, Ellie got to her feet. She turned to Jasper, and held up a small gun. It was tiny, a polished and engraved Derringer.

"Ellie." Jasper jumped back at the sight of the gun. He'd felt certain he was in no danger from her. "Hold on, now. There's no need for that."

"I want to be happy again."

"This ain't the way to make that happen. Put the gun down."

He finally had something real to live for, and Ellie had the power to end all of that in her small fingers.

She surprised the hell out of him when she swung the gun up and put it to her own temple.

"Dammit," Jasper said. "Ellie, don't you dare do something this stupid. You hurt enough people already."

"No one will be hurt by this."

"Charles will," Jasper said. He threw all the names he could at her. "Your folks—your ma will die without you. And what about Esther, and—for God's sake, Carolee needs someone to look up to. She's gonna have a baby. Don't you want to meet her baby? Charles is going to be mayor, I'm practically sure of it. Don't you want to be the mayor's wife?"

She shook as a sob came from her throat.

"Shut up," she hollered.

As she gestured, she moved the gun away from her head to do so. The moment it was pointed away, Hank came from seemingly nowhere and dove for her. He tackled her to the ground and landed hard enough to knock the gun out of her hand and have it scoot away. Jasper rushed forward and picked it up.

With Hank's size, it didn't take long for him to pin her arms behind her. Ellie only struggled for a moment, but there'd be no getting free of him. The fight went out of her and she wilted.

"We're taking you back to town."

"Are you going to tie my hands?"

Hank looked at Jasper for an answer to the strange question.

"Only to keep you from hurting yourself," he said.

"I don't want anyone to see me with tied hands."

"I'm sorry," Jasper said. Truly, he was. Appearance was everything to her, and having her town see her as a prisoner likely struck her right in the heart. Jasper pulled a small piece of rope from his saddlebag and tied her wrists as gently as he could. Then Hank put her on his horse, and took the lead line. He walked, and Jasper rode, and they led Ellie back to town.

She didn't say a word the whole way.

Jasper watched her, but she never changed expression.

The woman was broken somewhere deep inside. He'd known she had a mean streak, but never had he seen or imagined the depth of her pain. When he thought back, he couldn't remember the last time he'd heard her laugh, a real laugh and not one designed to sting.

She'd nearly killed him. She'd nearly killed Callie.

And all Jasper could muster for her was pity.

CHAPTER TWENTY~SEVEN

Callie

Hullabaloo woke Callie at sunrise, though she'd only slept an hour or two. Nate was still peaceful, so she moved him into the center of the cot and stepped out onto the boardwalk. She had meant to stay awake until the men returned from going after Ellie, but the night had caught up with her and she'd fallen into a sleep absent of dreams.

Jasper was helping Ellie down from Hank's horse. Ellie stood, and she walked, but seemed strange and lifeless. Her eyes grazed over Callie, but there was no recognition. Even the mean glint in her eyes seemed extinguished. She let Jasper lead her toward the jail, but he didn't bring her inside and put her into a cell.

With incredible gentleness, Jasper sat her in the rocking chair just outside the jail.

Hank followed a few steps behind. There was real concern on his face.

"What happened?" Callie asked. "Are you going to arrest her?"

Luke looked to Jasper. "This is your call, Deputy."

Jasper shook his head. "She's got something in her head that ain't right. What she did was criminal and stupid and dangerous, I know, but what good is her being in prison going to do?"

"What do you think?" Luke threw the question to Hank.

"Don't arrest her," he urged.

Callie heard both men's concern. She hadn't been with them, but two of the strongest men she'd ever met appeared shaken to their very bones. "What happened out there?"

"She tried to kill herself," Hank said softly. "Right in front of us."

Callie felt her rage melt away. At her lowest point, she'd never considered ending her life. Ellie had called her unhappy, but it was clear now that the unhappiness was her own. A lifetime of unhappiness and pretense had led her to this—and in the aftermath, she sat still, her face devoid of anything.

"Find Charles," Callie said. "Talk to him. He's got all the money in the world. He can take her away and get her some help, if that's what she needs."

"You're forgiving her?" Luke seemed surprised.

"Ain't that how mercy goes? She could never forgive me for my sins, so I'll forgive her hers. Despite everything she's done, I don't hate her." Callie leaned over to Ellie. "Do you hear me? I don't hate you."

The sheriff didn't seem convinced. "She could have hurt a lot of people."

"And it was a miracle she didn't." The sound of a commotion in the street made them all turn to look. Charles Graham rushed down the street toward his wife.

Luke stepped down the steps and intercepted him. "Mr. Graham."

Charles looked a fright. His normally slicked hair was mussed, his shirt was untucked, and he hadn't shaved. He'd clearly come directly from slumber at the news.

"What happened to Ellie? Is she all right?"

Luke shook his head. "She's safe, but she ain't all right."

Charles swallowed hard. "Can I see her?"

"Of course." Luke gestured with his head. Charles glanced past him and saw Ellie. He shook his head, then went to Ellie and dropped to a knee before her and took her hand in his. Her face was blank, dead.

"She started the fire," Jasper said. Someone had to say it.

Charles looked aghast. "My Ellie wouldn't—"

"She did, Charles. There's no question."

Every emotion any man had ever felt flickered past Charles's face. His lips twisted in anger, then his eyes watered, and finally he just put Ellie's hands to his lips. "I will take responsibility."

"That's not—"

"It is my responsibility. I may not have lit the match, but I sure as hell didn't set my foot down hard long ago and tell her to stop acting like a spoiled child."

Luke looked at Jasper, who nodded. "I won't arrest her, if you have someplace she can go."

Charles thought for a moment. "I have a sister in Denver. We'll go there for a while."

Denver was a fine city, the kind of place with big hospitals and plenty of doctors and not just the kind that tended to broken bones. There were places for people like Ellie, people with breaks in their minds and souls. Her going there, and far away from the daily sight of Jasper, would likely be the best thing.

Charles stood up and addressed Callie. "Miss Lee—Mrs. Tanner, I believe I should say."

"I'm gonna have to get used to that myself."

"I want to tell you especially how sorry I am for what happened."

"Well, thank you, Mr. Graham. It ain't hardly—"

"I'm dropping out of the race for mayor."

"But you're winning. Ellie said—"

"No, I'm not. The race is close, but I'm fairly certain you were ahead of me until you dropped out. And I'm glad for it. I think someone who has changed their life and made it better, and who has a family they love, is better suited for the task than I am."

"I appreciate that, Mr. Graham."

"Can you call me Charles?"

"Of course I can."

Charles looked at Luke. "I heard Deputy Frank was hurt."

"He took in a lot of smoke," Luke answered. "Doc thinks he'll be all right. He'll have to take it easy for a couple days."

"And Delia?"

"A couple burns, but she'll make it as well."

"I'll get her home," Charles said. "If anyone needs anything. Any money or…tell them to talk to me."

"I will pass that along."

Charles leaned down and whispered something in Ellie's ear for a moment. Carefully, he helped her up and away down the street, keeping an arm around her waist and her hand in his.

"That poor man," Luke said. "He has all the money in the world, and it won't help him at all. He'll have a tough time of it."

"Denver is a good idea," Hank said.

"Will George and Laura go with her, I wonder?"

"Things change, I suppose."

Wandering away from her friends, Callie reached the place where the doors of the saloon had been. The wood had been carved with star-shaped holes, two on each door. She remembered a hundred times standing by the doors, hooking her finger into one of the stars to pull or push the door. Every damn board would need to be rebuilt, and everything that had been inside replaced. Not a thing had survived undamaged.

All that remained were charred boards, a bunch of black ash, and the glass and metal that hadn't been melted by the fire. Callie knelt down and picked up a black-burnt round piece of wood. It had been a leg from one of the chairs at one of the tables, all of which were now destroyed.

Footsteps grew close. From one glance at the

black boots, she knew who stood beside her.

She held up the piece of wood. "From your hand-carved chairs."

"I ordered those from a man over in Austin."

"It's all gone." If anyone would understand the ache in her soul at seeing her beloved saloon in ashes, it would be Hank. The place had been his once, and he'd reveled in it the same way she had. "Jeepers. What am I gonna do?"

He crouched beside her. "You will rebuild it."

"With what?" she asked. "I don't have that kind of money. The money I did have went up in smoke last night along with everything else I've ever owned. The red dress too. Though that's probably a blessing."

From Hank's shirt pocket, he pulled a folded paper. "You may recall that when you and I left Fort Worth that day, I took some things that weren't entirely mine."

"You're not talking about Emma's money."

"No," he answered. "I gave her back her share and sent her off to marry her cowboy."

"She did, you know. Went to Laredo, married Bill, and then marched the McKenzie boys up here for a visit this spring. I swear, they acted better than choirboys."

He handed the paper to her. When she unfolded it, she saw the tops of bills.

"This is my share, and I want you to have it. For you, and for Nate, and for the fact that I've been a terrible son of a bitch all my life and I want to change that. Rebuild the saloon, Callie."

"I can't take this."

"Yes, you can. And you need to be strong, 'cause you're the mayor now and folks are going to look to you."

"When did you get so god-damned saintly?"

Hank laughed. It was a nice sound.

"Mama!"

Nate jumped onto her back, and Callie half-groaned as she laughed and tried not to fall over. Hooking her hands around his knees, she rose up with him in a piggyback.

"It's a damned mess, ain't it?" Jasper stepped up to them and looked at the remains.

"No one got hurt," Callie reminded him, then tipped to the side as Nate tried to climb down. Jasper swung the little boy in a circle, then set him down on the ground a few steps away from the rubble.

Callie saw Hank watching the interaction.

"You're good with him."

Jasper grinned. "Hard not to be. He's a good boy."

Hank looked at his feet. "Mr. Tanner, I want you to know I appreciate all you've done for Callie and for Nate. You've been the man and the father that I could never have been even if I'd been here and wanted to."

"Thank you?"

"If Nate were to call you daddy, I wouldn't be upset."

That was huge coming from Hank. Jasper looked ready to faint.

"Geez, Hank. Thank you. That means a lot. I knew this was going to be…"

"Awkward?"

"I was going to say goddamned awkward…"

"That works just as well."

"But you should know I bear you no ill will. You saved a few of us, and for that I think I think we owe you thanks. Far as I can tell, you're a scoundrel, but not a mean one."

"That might be the nicest thing anyone has ever said to me."

Callie couldn't keep from laughing.

CHAPTER
TWENTY-EIGHT

Hank

After everything settled, Hank passed the rest of the afternoon sleeping. Every muscle in his body hurt, he had cuts and a few minor burns that the good Doc Gray had tended to, and by the time he reached his room at the hotel and fell into his comfortable enough bed, his eyes were determined to close.

When he woke, he started for the saloon out of habit before he remembered the saloon was no more, and all that was left was a pile of charred boards.

"If you want a drink, you're going to probably have to go for a ride."

Haven stood on a stool, washing the outside wall of the clinic next door to the hotel. Her white rag was coming back gray. Even the businesses and buildings that hadn't burned outright had felt the effects of the fire.

She'd called out to him.

He went toward her, figuring she'd throw the rag at him.

"How's Matthew?"

"He's inside, sleeping. He'll be all right. I wanted to stay with him but Doc ordered me to go get some rest."

"Obviously you didn't listen."

"I tried. But I couldn't sleep. So I put myself to work. How are you?"

"Alive to see another day."

By then, he was only one step away from her. Haven stepped off her stool, dropped her rag in the bucket of water, and came to him. Her arms encircled him, her cheek rested on his shoulder, and he embraced her back.

The woman he loved more than any other was in his arms at last, and it was for reasons he'd never expected. It was not the embrace of passion, but of thanks.

And it was enough.

"Thank you," she breathed. "Thank you for saving him, though it was a damned stupid thing to do. You could have been killed yourself."

"It was for you. I could not bear the thought of you losing him," Hank confessed.

Haven smirked. "And here I thought you liked him."

Hank chuckled. Haven broke the embrace, stepping back.

"Were there bluebonnets this spring?"

"Millions."

"Did you collect any?"

"Not this time around. I didn't much feel like it. The world changes us, Hank. I might never be back to the girl I was back then, but maybe it's better that way."

"I'll always be here for you."

"Will you? Are you staying?"

He'd always be the odd man out. He'd always have to see Haven with Matthew, and Callie and Jasper with Nate. It was likely the sheriff would never really trust him. But still, the town was home. Every single person was going to need to pick up the pieces and rebuild their lives, and there was no reason he couldn't do it as well.

"I'm sticking around," he decided. He shoved his hands in his pockets like a nervous schoolboy, hoping she'd approve. "I figure I've run out on enough people who needed me through the years. Maybe it's about time I settled down somewhere, and I can't think of anywhere better."

"Your son is here."

Hank nodded. "He's Jasper's son, and it's fine by me if he grows up thinking that. I'll be here for him if he needs me, and for Callie, who I still feel like I would face an army to protect. And you, of course. Maybe you most of all."

"If you're hoping I'll cast aside my husband and run into your rascal arms, you need to ride the hell out of here right now."

"I'm not hoping for that," he said. "I'm just hoping that, should you ever have need of a friend, you'd think of me."

"I bet I could do that."

"Don't start talking about betting." He shook his

head and looked to where the saloon had been. "I have no doubt that once I come to my senses I'll be restless and desirous of a gambling hall."

"There's always Greeley."

Hank rolled his eyes. "Amateurs."

"With Charles and Ellie headed to Denver, he's selling the hotel, you know."

"So?"

"So a man who has traveled as much as you have, and likes the finer things the way you do, might be just the right person to buy it. Or is that putting down too many roots, too fast?"

He wagged a finger at her. "You're trouble, Mrs. Frank."

"You would know."

Hank Porter, hotelier. He saw an image of himself, finely dressed and greeting new arrivals from the front doors of the finest hotel in east Texas. He could spiff up the place, make it fancier, and he could even put in a small bar of his own. He had to chuckle at the idea of being rivals with Callie. She'd skin him alive.

He turned away from Haven.

"Where are you off to?"

"Why, Mrs. Frank, I appear to be headed off to see a man about a hotel."

"I figured."

"Although if you ever do feel like running off with me, you know where to find me."

"The nearest card game?" she asked, and he laughed. "You will be the death of me, Hank."

"Probably."

"You should probably send for one of those

mail-order brides," she said. She picked up her rag again and stepped back up onto her stool. "A woman not from around here, who didn't know any of us from a hill of beans, might just take to you. You have your appealing traits, you know."

"Oh, do I?"

She flicked the rag at him, and water splattered his face. "Oh, go buy a hotel."

"I think I will," he said. "Fix it up, make it shine, and then maybe after that I'll get myself a mail-order bride like you said."

"You wouldn't."

"I would, indeed."

"The poor woman." Haven beamed, then turned back to her task.

CHAPTER TWENTY-NINE

Callie

For most of her patrons, Callie served up good whiskey—none of the watered-down stuff.

For Doctor Cornelius Gray, she served the especially good stuff. It didn't happen often that Doc visited the saloon, but sometimes—and she knew it was only on the days when his work at his clinic was too much for a mortal man to handle—he bellied up to the bar next to Hill and the boys. On those occasions, she ducked down to the back of a shelf below the bar and pulled out a bottle of Kentucky whiskey she'd ordered especially for him.

Doc deserved it, every drop.

He'd brought Nate into this world, and helped Callie through her pregnancy without so much as one judgmental comment about her being unwed, or the father of her child being a long-gone gambler. That wasn't Doc's way, to judge.

And after he'd done it, Callie had ordered him a

bottle of the good stuff and given it to him, wrapped with a bow. So it was that, five nights after the fire had gone out and all was quiet again, Doc offered up the bottle and she called everyone out to supper at the Tanner house.

They couldn't give Jack Braxton a funeral. His body was somewhere in Tennessee, buried somehow under who knew what kind of conditions. But they could gather and remember him.

Haven made dinner, teaching Callie one of her recipes. Cooking a nightly dinner for a family was a skill Callie knew she'd need to master, and fast. They ate, and they talked, and it was a nice evening.

After dinner, Callie made them all go out onto the porch.

The sky was full of stars, and the breeze was just a bit chilly.

"Jasper," she said.

He leapt to his task, and handed each of them a shot glass.

"I'd like to thank Doc for his generosity." She held up the whiskey bottle.

"Oh Lord," Haven said.

"There's no one else I'd rather share my libations with."

Callie poured each of her friends a drink, then one for herself.

"If you'll indulge me, I'd like to say something."

"Go on," Luke urged.

"Jack wasn't a man who liked to talk to everyone. He was irritable, foul-mouthed, and I swear he disliked more people than he liked in this world. But he was also kind, and a good man, and underneath it all he had a good heart. It's a real shame he wound up the way he did. I wish we could give him a burial here, but since we can't—"

She choked up. Jasper slipped a hand around her waist.

Luke took over, raising his glass. "To Braxton, the grumpy bastard."

"To Braxton." Everyone raised their glasses and drank.

Haven coughed at the strong drink. "I still can't believe you all drink this stuff on purpose."

"I think we all have memories of him," Luke said. "Anyone feel like sharing?"

"I pulled a knife out of his leg," Haven said. "And he was rude to me. And then he saved my life a few times, so bless him—wherever he wound up."

"He went with me out to the McKenzie drive," Matthew said. "Two days of riding, and he said maybe five words the whole time. And I was grateful for it."

"The first time I…met him…" They all knew how she and Braxton had met. "He had that scraggly beard and that long hair. I told him if he wanted to spend time with me he needed to go get cleaned up. And I about fainted when he came back and he had."

"I wouldn't be standing here without him," Luke said.

"He liked good whiskey," Doc said. "He'd have liked this."

They all stood in silence.

"It feels wrong that Porter isn't here," Matthew said.

"You feeling all right?" Callie asked.

"Matthew is right," Luke said. "I haven't seen him since the fire. Is he still around?"

"He's around," Haven said. "He's staying."

"You believe him?" Luke asked.

She nodded. "This time I do."

On the way into the house, Luke put his hands on Callie's shoulders. "The best thing you can do to honor Braxton is to live a good life and be happy. That's what he wanted for you. I truly believe it."

"I think so too."

"He's probably looking down at you from the stars right now."

Callie pursed her lips. "I think we both know he just as likely wound up in the other place."

Devil or angel, Braxton had gone away. But like any member of a family who passes on, he wouldn't be forgotten. Callie liked the name Jack. Maybe she'd name her next son Jack, as a tribute.

In case he was up there watching, she winked at the stars.

CHAPTER THIRTY

Jasper

Two weeks later, after a shipment of lumber had arrived via a number of wagons ordered through Harper's store, Callie and Jasper stood in the cleared spot where the saloon had stood.

In his hands, Jasper held the plans for the new saloon. Between the two of them, Delia Lance, and Ira Henderson, and Hill's impressive art skills, there had been sketches that had then been turned into plans to rebuild the businesses that had only recently stood where they now set foot.

"You sure you don't want an upstairs on the new place?" he said with a shrug.

"There's no reason for one anymore," she said. "I won't hire any girls, and I won't be living up there. I need more storage behind the bar more than I need empty bedrooms."

"Well, this shouldn't be too hard." It would be a hell of a lot of work, but nothing they couldn't do with a good number of dedicated people, which they certainly had.

The town had rallied behind their new mayor as she'd led the charge.

Callie held up a hammer. "Let's get to work."

She'd tied her hair back in a tail, and wore a set of Jasper's clothes. The shirt was too big on her, and the pants had to be held up with one of his belts, but he thought she'd never looked better. There wasn't time to let the thoughts in his head turn passionate, though.

Callie went directly to a pile of boards. For two weeks, she'd been itching to get to work rebuilding. She'd settled into living at Jasper's place, but without her saloon she'd been jittery. Finally, the day of the building bee had finally arrived. Her first act as mayor had been to declare it a community project, and to ask for the townspeople's help to rebuild the three structures and the damaged section of the bathhouse. Gallons of lemonade and a multitude of cookies and pies sat ready to repay the folks who decided to lend hands to the project.

"You startin' without us?"

The Tanners turned around to find Hill Hilton, Ed Dean, and Rip Piper behind them. All three of the men carried tools in their hands.

"Boys." Callie was truly touched. "You don't have to do this."

"I held that bar up for years," Hill said. "I aim to do the same for a few more."

Luke and Doc walked up together. "Don't know about you, Doc, but I feel like building something."

"I'm not much for building, but I'll be here for when someone inevitably smashes a thumb with a hammer or gets a splinter." Doc winked at Callie.

Matthew approached with a person in pants. It took Jasper a minute to realize it was Haven, wearing her husband's clothes, though the pants' hems and shirt sleeves had to be rolled up. "Look at you," Jasper commended her.

"I can saw and hammer as well as any man," she said. As if it were proof, she held up a saw nearly as long as her arm.

Jasper stepped back with a laugh. "I don't doubt it."

"Look alive." Doc pointed down the street.

A whole passel of rough-looking riders approached, riding at a run. Dust kicked up behind them, and people rushed out of the way.

"Those cowboys are about to be sorely disappointed," Luke said.

"I don't think they are," Matthew said slowly. "Look who's up front."

The riders were, indeed, cowboys, but they were no strangers. It was the McKenzie boys: Bill, Jess, Pete, and Saul, likely coming from their ranch in Laredo. In the past, the McKenzies arriving in town would have made all the lawmen go for their guns to ward off a city-wide street brawl before it began, but no more. Bill McKenzie, the eldest brother, had put a stop to the trouble the previous spring. Jasper liked the man, and knew Matthew and Luke did too.

Bill was riding with the group, but he wasn't leading them.

Out in front, riding strong and smiling all the while, was a flame-haired beauty in trail clothes.

Emma Porter McKenzie whooped and waved. Every one of them wore a smile as they got closer.

"Hot damn," Matthew cried. "The cavalry came."

"What on Earth?" Callie called as she ran toward them.

Bill shook his head at the empty space where the buildings had stood. "Looks like you misplaced part of your town." He dismounted and shook Matthew's hand immediately. "Deputy."

"What in the hell are you doing here?" Callie asked, speaking up to Emma.

"Hank wired us," Emma said. "He told us what happened. So we all got together and figured if you were gonna be building that you might need some extra hands for a few days."

"You bet we can," Jasper said.

"We're here to work," Bill said.

"Your timing couldn't be better," Matthew said. "Every pair of hands helps."

"So let's do it."

Work began right then and there. The McKenzie boys were used to hard work with their hands, and jumped in like it was their own place they were building. Jasper and Matthew led the construction part of the operation, and within two hours' time the layout of all the beams to be built for each wall and part of the three buildings was in place and actual building was already beginning.

* * *

Callie

Emma took a break from measuring and sawing

263

boards to get a drink of water, and Callie slipped off to speak to her in private.

"So you married him," Emma said with a studying glance at Jasper.

"I did," Callie said.

"Good on you," Emma replied. "I knew you were crazy about each other."

Callie swatted her.

"And you." Emma turned to Haven, who had come up between them both. "How are you?"

Callie realized the last time Emma and Haven had met, Haven had been ready to burst with child. Haven embraced Emma. "I will be all right."

"We're all gonna be all right," Callie said.

The three women looked toward the construction, where the men were hammering and sawing boards into the frame that would start the outline of the new saloon.

"Look at those boys." Emma grinned. "I could stand and watch Bill all day."

"He ain't bad to look at," Callie agreed.

"Yours either," Emma said. "And red-haired men aren't usually my thing, but my goodness. Jasper fills out a pair of pants like—"

"Watch your mouth," Callie warned. "I don't want to have to mention how fine Bill's—"

"You two!" Haven shrieked. "You're no better than they are!"

Emma's laugh came loud and hearty. "Speaking of good-looking, where's my no-account ex-husband?"

In that moment, Callie realized she hadn't seen Hank in a day or two. After everything that had happened, could Hank have slipped away from Cricket Bend yet again? He seemed to have changed so much, to have made a place—or started to—that he could call home.

Jeepers. She would miss him.

"Mrs. McKenzie!"

There was that slight lilt, that hint of a southern drawl spoken in a smooth baritone. Hank came toward the trio grinning hugely, probably at the sight of the three of them all standing together. Lord, but the four of them could write a book, or three, or even four, about the times they'd had, and the red dress they'd all worn at one time or another. A dress that now lay in ashes, though it was probably an appropriate ending.

Emma turned it on, the way she always did for Hank. "Porter, I figured by now you'd be six feet under up in the Klondike or the like."

"It's cold in the Klondike," he retorted. "Why in the hell would I go there?"

"Makes about as much sense as you being here."

"Do you and your cowboys require a place to stay? I hear tell there are still some rooms left at the hotel."

"I'll speak with the owner."

"You're speaking with him right now."

Callie squealed. "You didn't."

"I got a tip that it was for sale. You told me you were going to turn this town into something, Mayor Lee. I took you at your word, in the hopes that the hotel could become a profitable investment. Don't let me down." He winked at her.

"Do I ever?"

"We've got a special rate for friends who've come to town to help with the rebuilding," Hank said. "Zero dollars a night."

"Then I'll take three rooms," Emma said.

"Excellent. I trust your cowboys won't make trouble."

"Nothing you can't handle."

Laughing, Hank left them and went toward the construction.

Matthew saw him approaching, and held out a hammer. Hank took it. The two men conferred for a moment, then Hank went to join in the lifting of four beams nailed together to create the frame of a wall.

"Did he really buy the hotel?" Emma asked.

Haven nodded. "Yep. He sure did."

Callie scooped herself a cup of water from the barrel. "I'll be damned. He's going legitimate."

"To Hank Porter." Emma raised her glass. Haven laughed, but did the same. Callie did too. "The only man who could make a small-town hotel into an adventure."

The three women clinked their cups and sipped their drinks.

"You ladies plannin' to sit over there lookin' pretty or come do some actual work?" Bill McKenzie teased from atop a wagon full of boards.

"I like the view from here," Emma called back to him. "Turn back around, would you?"

The three women walked across the street. Bill bent down and whispered something to Emma that made her smack him. Matthew pulled Haven to him and kissed the top of her head. Saul McKenzie, off to the side of the group, started to play a tune on a harmonica.

Callie smiled at the sight of the people she loved happy.

A few yards away, the ones she loved most were together. Jasper knelt with Nate, pointing at something on the plan. The little boy pointed excitedly at something, and reached for a big nail, but Jasper plucked it out of his hand just the way a father would.

He saw her looking back, and grinned that sweet smile of his. Callie breathed a sigh of contentment. They would be fine, the lot of them.

Cricket Bend would be just fine.

The End

ACKNOWLEDGEMENTS

Writing a trilogy is insane. It's time-consuming and exhausting, and yet incredibly thrilling and fun at the same time. Without the encouragement of a whole slew of people, this wouldn't have happened. I am forever grateful to my husband, son, and cats who allowed me to lock myself away and type like a madwoman—they're my heroes.

Thank you to my parents, Aleisha, Megan, Annie and Ryan, Amanda, Harley Easton, Trysh Thompson, Bob, Chris, all the fine and filthy ladies of my book club, and everyone who ever came out to celebrate these books.

If you're a fan of Western Historical Romance, join the lively discussion at Pioneer Hearts.

https://www.facebook.com/groups/pioneerhearts/

ABOUT THE AUTHOR

Marie Piper earned her B.A. in English Literature from Michigan State University. She lives in Chicago where she enjoys coffee, history, nature, and surrounding herself with her ever-expanding book hoard. Marie's short stories have appeared in collections from LoveSlave, House of Erotica, Coming Together, NineStar Press, and Insatiable Press. Her five-novella western historical mystery serial, MAIDENS & MONSTERS, will conclude in April 2017.

Facebook:
https://www.facebook.com/MariePiperBooks

Twitter:
https://twitter.com/mariepiperbooks

Website:
http://www.mariepiper.com/

Goodreads:
https://www.goodreads.com/MariePiper